Snowed Inn

ERIN BRANSCOM

Snowed Inn

Freedom Valley Series

Copyright © 2024 by Erin Branscom

Erin Branscom
www.erinbranscom.com

ISBN: 979-8-88662-020-7 (paperback)

Editor: Emerald Edits and Editing 4 Indies
Cover Design and formatting: Yummy Book Covers

*For Aunt Susan, thanks for being one of the
strongest and wisest women I know.
We hit the auntie lottery when we got you.*

Snowed Inn

CHAPTER 1

Holly

"I'm sorry, what did you just say?" I frantically scan the empty classroom and look for a place to steady myself from the shocking news I just received from the person on the phone. I lean back, my body trembling as I prop myself up against the densely decorated wall adorned with my kids' artwork. My face, no doubt, a stark contrast of gray to the multitude of colors on display.

"I'm very sorry, Holly. This isn't the outcome the agency or the family could ever have foreseen. We're a newer and smaller local agency, and we've never had this happen. Since we no longer have a family available, there are options for you to consider. You have the option of keeping your biological baby, or we can place it in the foster care system."

It. This baby is *not* an *it.* Anger begins to fill me like lava. It's a baby, not an object. The baby is a human being and will *not* be going into the foster care system. Over my dead body. Surely, there's another option. When I signed up to be a surrogate, this was not how I imagined this would go. This baby was adored and wanted by the family, and now they're gone...and my heart shatters as I process this.

"What about any family members?" I ask, still shocked. Fortunately, the couple's older child is safe, but I'm shocked that the couple I bonded with is gone, and now no one can take their baby.

"Unfortunately, the surviving family members are not able to take the baby, and we're still working out all the details with our attorney. The agency doesn't have another family to consider at this time. We'll help you navigate whichever option you decide," the case manager repeats grimly. My heart sinks as this information soaks in, feeling heavier by the minute.

"Again, we're very sorry. We'll be in touch." He sounds just as uncomfortable as I am, delivering this life-changing blow as he quickly disconnects from the phone call.

My heart shatters for the excited parents, who I've just been told died last week in a boating accident while on vacation, and I feel like my world is caving in. What am I supposed to do now? And who delivers news like this to someone while they're in the middle of their workday?

My hands cover my face, and I rub my temple with my fingers. I feel a pressure headache coming on as I try to hold back the tears being held by a dam threatening to leak by the second. I don't know what to do with all this information. It's too much. I have about twenty third graders who I'm responsible for who are about to come in from recess to a teacher about to have a mental breakdown. And a mental breakdown was not on the list for today. No, I was supposed to finish up my day teaching and head over to the bookstore for tea and bookshelf stocking with Paige. I don't have time for this bomb just casually dropped on me out of nowhere.

My heart sank when the case manager said the couple's guardian is the grandparents, who are in their seventies and not in the place to take on a new baby along with the couple's older child. And I get it. *But I don't get it.* This hasn't been my baby. The baby was always theirs. I never could have prepared myself for this scenario, and now I'm just wrecked. I'm not even sure I know the words for the feelings that I'm having right now. When the case manager said I could put the baby in the system, I immediately knew I could never do that. My friend Beth grew up in the foster care system, and her stories have shocked and saddened me for every kid who has experienced that. Legally, this is a shit show, and whatever happens, it's not going to change the fact that there's a baby now who needs me.

My baby.

My hand covers my mouth, and I gulp a deep breath to hold back a sob as I swipe hot tears before they pour down my face. I pause to feel for the baby to kick or move, to make sure the baby is okay. "Come on, give me something," I murmur. My hand moves to my stomach, rubbing it gently.

My heart breaks for the family. The parents who couldn't conceive again and counted on me to complete their beautiful family. They were over the moon excited for the baby, and they lived for the weekly updates we shared. When the update went unanswered last week, I knew something had to be wrong. It wasn't like them not to respond to my email. And the news I just received about them devastates me.

Ready or not, this baby is coming in the next few months, and I'm not prepared. This was supposed to be a labor of love for all of us. I was helping a family achieve their dream of becoming parents again. Something I had thought long and hard about so I could also help my own future family's legacy. My *future* family. Like *way* in the future. I'm only twenty-seven and don't feel ready to become a mom. I'm single, and this was not how it was supposed to go. I haven't told anyone except my best friend Ophelia about the surrogacy. No one even knows. I was keeping this to myself and hoping to deliver the baby quietly and go back to my life afterward. How will I explain to my family and friends how I suddenly had a baby?

Surprise! You're suddenly grandparents to my sperm donor baby that I intended to give away to another family? Oh, yeah, and even though you already accused me of being too irresponsible, I did all this to buy back the family restaurant you sold to someone else?

All of that makes me sound and feel like a crazy person. Oh my God. What if I am crazy?

We were supposed to be helping each other, and I was counting on the money from the surrogacy to start rebuilding my family's restaurant. Now I'll be a single mom with no home or stable job. I need to contact my lawyer, Preston Steele, before I do anything else. Ultimately, I need to protect this baby at all costs. This baby won't be going into foster care. That's the only thing I know for sure right now.

Everything just changed in an instant for me. My perfect plan is now gone. The rug has been ripped out from under me.

Oh God, what have I done?

This has all backfired.

The baby I've worked so hard not to bond with and tried to pretend isn't real, to protect my heart, all of a sudden feels *very* real.

The door to the classroom slams open, rattling the glass as the kids noisily file into the classroom after recess. I sink down on the floor, feeling woozy, waiting for this gut punch of emotions I just received to pass. I swallow and take a deep breath and try to smile so I don't freak the kids out who I'm substituting for right now. But these eight-year-olds are intuitive, and they know something is up. I'm not convincing any of them that everything is okay. The fake maniac-looking joker smile I have plastered on my face probably looks scarier than me just sitting here quietly panicking.

"You don't look so good, Miss Springs," Toby, one of my students, calls out, wrinkling his nose up at me in disgust.

Why do these kids always have to be so brutally honest?

Another student peers over Toby at me. "She looks really weird like when my little sister puked—"

I hold up my hand. "No! Don't finish that sentence," I blurt out as I take deep breaths and scan the room as I battle out this nausea. The room suddenly feels like it's spinning.

"I wonder what color it will be…" another kid pipes in.

I look up at the ceiling and gulp deep breaths.

Pull it together, Holly.

I'm responsible for these tiny humans. I desperately think of a way to focus and not pass out. I stare up at the bright-colored vocabulary words on the wall. *Focus.*

The room continues to spin, and so many colors move so fast. I pull at the neck of my sweatshirt. It feels so hot in here. I can't breathe. Am I having a panic attack? Maybe I'm dying. I've officially worked myself to death. My hand goes to my abdomen protectively. *No…*

And that's the last thought that runs through my head before everything stops.

CHAPTER 2

Holly

I open my eyes and instinctively reach for my belly, worry consuming me. I blink at a handsome man's bright green eyes peering down at me. I must be dreaming because I've never seen this man before, and he's up close and personal. And right now, it feels very personal. I'm on the floor, and he's gazing into my eyes as he kneels before me.

"Am I dreaming?" I whisper as I struggle to get up.

"There she is," the man says confidently, squeezing my hand reassuringly as he helps me sit up.

I'm still on the floor in the classroom, but the kids are gone. I can see and hear them through the window having an extra recess, which I'm sure they're not mad about. How long did I pass out? Guilt fills me. I hope I didn't scare or worry the kids. I scan the playground and see the next-door teacher supervising all the kids and looking back at me through the window with concern as she talks to the assistant principal.

"Can you tell me your name?" The young paramedic breaks my thoughts as he slides a blood pressure cuff on me. He pushes a few buttons, and it begins to squeeze my arm.

"Holly," I whisper nervously as my hand goes straight to my belly bump. *The baby.* My small round bump is still there and hidden under my baggy sweatshirt that says "Let's get Saucy" with a piece of dancing pizza on it. I wore it because it makes the kids laugh. Most of them know me from going to my family's pizza restaurant that we used to own in town called Freedom Pie. I grew up and worked there until recently when my parents decided to up and sell it and retire to sunny Florida. And despite their pleas for me to move to Florida with them to their retirement community, which I politely refused, this hasn't gone well for me, and I've been trying to get my head above water for months now.

I've been working as many part-time jobs as I can to save up to open my own restaurant. I may have lost my dream of owning Freedom Pie, but I have a plan. *Had a plan.* Well, that's all gone to shit now. Substitute teaching being one of them, along with being a surrogate, stocking bookshelves at the bookstore for Paige, helping Ophelia groom dogs, and my secret black market pizza pop-up shops that my friend

Allie lets me conduct out of the back alley of her bakery.

Luckily, I've saved up some money, but I'm still far from being able to buy the restaurant back from the new owners or start over with a new shop. I would really like to buy it back since I don't know if the new owners will last. I read and researched, and statistically, new restaurants have a hard time the first year, and from what I've been hearing, it hasn't been going well. Their pizza tastes terrible. I still don't agree with my parents' reasoning on why they wouldn't let me buy it. We had a huge argument. They didn't think I should tie myself to the pizza place for life like they did. I'd argued that they shouldn't have decided that for me.

Do I want the new owner to fail? Yes and no. I want my restaurant back but don't necessarily want someone else's business to fail. I'm in the good karma business, not the bad karma business. I'm not wishing that on anyone. I've come to terms with the fact that I'll probably just have to start over. I've never wanted something so badly in my life. It never should have been sold to anyone else in the first place, let alone two old men who probably know nothing about pizza. Pizza has been my life for twenty-seven years and is in my bones. I want it back. I need it back.

Exhaustion fills me as I lean my head against the front of the teacher's desk and close my eyes. The restaurant is the least of my worries now. I have a baby to plan for. *Holy shit.*

The paramedic clears his throat, bringing me back to

reality. "I'm Hank, a firefighter and paramedic, but today, I'm just your paramedic," he jokes as he makes notes on a tablet in a thick black case. "No need for a fireman unless those kids have any plans."

"As bad as this day is going, I wouldn't be surprised if something burned down, too," I mutter.

A dimple pops on his cheek when he smiles at me as he leans down to look at the blood pressure reading. "Do you know where you are?"

Hell, I think as I look around. "Yes, at the school. I'm so sorry we had to bother you."

I just want to go home and curl up in my bed and have a good cry. I have a lot of things to figure out.

"It's alright, it happens. Any medical conditions?" he asks, and the softness of his voice makes my chest squeeze.

I look around, and I swallow and nod. Now I'm worried about the baby. Everything has to be okay...I can't let anything happen to the baby.

"What's going on?" he asks, compassion washing over his face.

"I'm pregnant. I was trying to keep it a secret," I whisper. "I'm worried about the baby. I've never passed out before."

"How far along are you?" he asks as he sits back on his heels, his shiny black shoes and tight navy cargo pants distracting me from looking at his striking green eyes. He rummages through his bag and pulls out a fetal Doppler, and

I raise my shirt slightly as he presses it to my belly.

"Thirty-two," I whisper softly as relief fills me when I hear the fast-paced heart rate.

He nods reassuringly, his kind eyes full of compassion. "We'll take a little ride and get you and your baby looked at. We'll get you taken care of," he says confidently as he stands.

Your baby.

Hearing that said out loud and the confirmation that this is, in fact, my baby now makes me feel anxious and emotionally heavy all over again. I suck in a deep breath and focus on calming down, so I don't pass out again. This stress isn't good for the baby.

"I need my phone," I murmur as I reach for it and realize that Lola, who I've known for years and must be Hank's partner, has set my coat, purse, and phone next to the stretcher. I'm so embarrassed that I passed out. Lola gives me a reassuring pat on the shoulder.

He turns, and his navy T-shirt with the Freedom Valley Fire Department emblem over his heart stretches tight across his chest, biceps bulging from the sleeves of his shirt as I watch him lift the gurney. The muscles in his forearms strain as he picks up the medical bag and hoists it over his shoulder. This is when I realize how strikingly handsome this man is. *Wow.* He has great thick, wavy dark brown hair that looks slightly overdue for a haircut. I won't lie and say I didn't dream of running my fingers through it. But his eyes are what are so striking. He's got the kindest green eyes. He could be a younger Patrick Dempsey with the whole *Grey's Anatomy* vibes going.

"I can walk..." I stammer as I move to swing my legs over. I don't want to ride in an ambulance and draw any more attention to myself. And the cost of this will set me back tremendously and eat into my savings.

"No, it's okay," he reassures me, laying a hand on my forearm. "I've got you."

He begins to push me out to the ambulance, and my heart clenches. I mentally kick myself for not getting enough rest last night. I was up late getting the pizza pop-up shop ready to go for this upcoming weekend when I should have been resting. I need to do better for this baby. For me, too.

I remember the call from the agency's case manager. I close my eyes and groan because that wasn't a dream. It was a real-life nightmare.

On the way to the hospital, Hank cracks a few jokes to make me smile. Surprisingly, it works. He does a good job of setting me at ease in a stressful situation. Despite my worry, he gets a smile out of me and seems like a nice guy. I can tell he likes his job and he's good with people. I appreciate the distraction from the dump truck–sized worry filling me by the minute.

"How long have you been a firefighter and paramedic?" I ask as I look over. He's buckled in the seat beside me, marking things off on a clipboard.

"Six years. My brother and I moved here last summer."

"Welcome to Freedom Valley," I murmur.

"Have you lived here long?" He looks over, his kind eyes sweeping over my shirt. "I like your shirt."

"I grew up here," I say proudly. "And thanks. My family used to own the pizza place in town, so pizza's kind of my thing." I smooth down my silly sweatshirt. Not sure why I feel the urge to explain this to him, but I do.

A funny look crosses his face, and his forehead wrinkles. "Did your family own Freedom Pie?"

"Yes, but it's sold now to two older brothers. Have you been there?"

He chuckles. "As a matter of fact, I have."

"Did you like it? I heard the new owners can't get the pizza right," I huff. "I've tried to buy it back, but they won't sell."

Before he can respond, I look up as I realize we've come to a stop. The door flies open, and the ambulance driver, Lola, appears with a smile. "Alright, less talk, more moving, Sutton." She's a no-nonsense woman, and I've known her all my life. She gives me a friendly smile, but it's all business. Relief fills me that she's not asking me more about my situation. Small towns are not the place to blend in and try to keep secrets. Everyone knows everyone and all their business. And I need everyone not to know my business right now.

"Thank you for your help, Hank," I call as he passes.

He puts his hand up. "Of course. I'll be right back."

Sutton. Why is that name so familiar?

CHAPTER 3

Holly

"There you are! You scared me to death!" my best friend Ophelia says as she stands outside the emergency room entrance with her arms crossed and worry etched on her face.

"How'd you know I was here?" I ask, confused as to why she's at the hospital but relieved to see her.

"You put me down as your emergency contact at the school," she says, shivering in her coat, wrapping her arms around her shoulders. "I was so worried when they called me." She's still wearing the black waterproof apron she wears when she grooms dogs at her shop. She must have come straight from work. Warmth fills me that she came for me. I smile at her gratefully. It feels good to have her here and not be alone. I've been feeling so alone lately, and I don't know what I'd do without Ophelia.

"I'm fine," I reassure her. "I just fainted. I must not have eaten enough today."

I reach down to make sure my baggy sweatshirt conceals my stomach, looking around at the busy emergency room entrance. She watches me and purses her lips. She hasn't been a fan of my surrogacy plan, but she's still been supportive every step of the way. She's been by my side through it all. I don't know what I would have done without her.

"Did you have to leave work? I'm sorry," I say as Lola pulls the gurney down, and it clicks into place.

I look over, and Hank is talking quietly with the nurses and motioning to me. He's focused as he turns and strolls over to grab the other end of the gurney. He pushes me inside as warmth hits me once we get through the hospital doors, and the smell of the hospital is a stark wake up to my situation.

At that moment, Hank turns and crashes into Ophelia, who has been quietly following us.

"Oh...I'm so sorry," she stammers, staring up into Hank's face, not breaking eye contact as she stands with her palms resting on his chest to steady herself. His hand lingers on her arm where he caught her when they crashed into each other. He's equally as entranced with her and staring back at her.

Hank has a slow grin, and his face softens as he doesn't

break eye contact with Ophelia. I watch this with fascination as they stare at each other with awkward grins frozen in place.

"Wow," she breathes. "You have really pretty eyes. Can I have them?" she jokes as she stares at him, completely mesmerized.

"No." He laughs and flashes a wink in her direction. "But your kids can."

Her eyes go wide, and she laughs nervously. Her eyes dart to me and then back to Hank. "My, my, aren't you the biggest flirt?"

"Only when I catch a pretty lady in my arms," he says with a wink.

I cover my mouth with a laugh, realizing I have just watched the most epic meet cute I've ever seen. Romance books couldn't top this. I'm going to give her so much crap about this later. And right now, I'm grateful for the distraction.

He finally turns to say something to Lola, and a stunned Opi mouths to me, "Where did he come from?"

I shrug and grin, rubbing my belly to get the baby to move. I'm not in pain, but I haven't felt movement since I passed out so that concerns me. Maybe the baby is napping. I'm relieved I'm here at the hospital to get checked out just in case.

I try to think of something to distract me as I watch Opi

stare after Hank. Well, well, well, Ophelia likes the hot firefighter. She hasn't shown any interest in dating since she swore off all men. Her loser ex-fiancé stole from her and a bunch of other people and skipped town, leaving her jaded and not trusting anyone, and I don't blame her. It's nice seeing her flirting again. She deserves better than what she had with shithead Nial. And what kind of name is Nial, anyway? I roll my eyes and shake my head, just thinking about that moron. If I ever see him again, God help him. He's dead meat to me after what he did to my best friend. She's had to start over completely, and some people in this town haven't been very nice to her. I've had to deal with some of them, too. Opi doesn't have any family other than her brother, Axel, so I look out for her.

I have to tell Opi about what happened with the surrogacy. She tried to talk me out of doing it in the first place. She won't say I told you so, but she was right. She didn't think it was a good idea and even offered to help me find a different way to get the money to open a new restaurant. She all but begged me not to do the surrogacy. Did I listen? Nope. And here we are.

The doctor walks into the bay, breaking up the epic meet cute between Opi and Hank, the paramedic. She smiles warmly with recognition when she sees me. *Callie.*

"Hi, Holly," she says in a friendly and professional voice despite us being friends. "Our paramedic updated me on your situation and told me it's confidential, which I can assure you it will be."

Relief fills me that it's Callie, the local town doctor who just married her high school sweetheart, SJ Reid, local mechanic and high school football coach. She's tall, has a long blond braid over her shoulder, and bright blue eyes. Even though I know her and know her well, she's still professional. I'm in good hands with her. But I know she's probably got a million questions about me and my situation.

"Hi, okay, thank you," I whisper nervously, looking around. This is the downside of living in a small town. Everyone knows everyone, and it's impossible to fly under the radar.

"What's going on?" she asks as she slides over on a stool and tucks her hands into the pockets of her white coat. She was always the nice, quiet, smart kid who dated the high school football player. Everyone knew SJ and Callie. Now, she's Dr. Reid.

I nervously look over at Hank and Ophelia, and he watches me, then turns and says to Ophelia, "I have a quick break. Would you like to grab a coffee with me?"

Ophelia looks like she wants to say no and glances at me hesitantly, but I nod that it's okay. "I will get all my paperwork filled out and get checked out. I'm fine."

"I'll be right back," Opi says as Dr. Reid waves to them and reaches over to pull the door shut as Hank guides her out.

"Says here you're in your third trimester," she says quietly, looking at my chart. "When did this happen? I had no idea."

"I'm a surrogate. Was a surrogate. I just found out that the surrogate family no longer will be taking the baby." I start to cry, and she reaches over and takes my hand.

She nods. "Did you just find that out today?"

I nod. "I was hoping I could pull this off quietly, and no one would find out." Unreasonable, maybe, but it was my plan.

Her blue eyes are full of compassion as she listens, nodding every so often and not saying anything.

"I just wanted to make money to start over with the restaurant," I say and realize it probably sounds selfish. Freedom Pie wasn't just my family's restaurant. It was my home and my passion, and I miss it very much. I was willing to do anything to get it back, including signing up to be a surrogate. I thought it was just nine months of work, and I'd have a down payment to start. I never imagined I'd set myself back even further financially and change the course of my life forever.

"The parents I was a surrogate for passed away in an accident," I add softly.

She listens and lays a hand on mine. "Who has been your support system?"

"Only Ophelia knows," I say, glancing at the door and wondering when she'll return.

"Well, let's take a look at the baby," she says as she pulls over the portable ultrasound machine. After shaking up a tube, she squirts the warm jelly liquid on my belly bump. She picks up the wand, places it on my stomach, and moves it around, pushing in slightly. I listen for the baby's heartbeat, and it picks up and beats quickly. Relief fills me as I turn my face away from the monitor screen out of habit, trying to tune it out like I normally do. I've trained myself not to pay attention when they check the baby at my appointments. I've pretended the photos and sounds aren't real so I won't get attached.

"How are your parents doing down in Florida?" She looks over at me, making me feel more like she's a friend than a doctor with her soft tone.

"They seem fine. They don't know either," I admit as I stare up and count the ceiling tiles to distract myself.

I sneak a quick glance over. She looks at me with a look I'm unable to read and then looks back at the monitor.

"Is the baby okay?" I whisper nervously.

"Baby looks amazing," she says. "Your pregnancy is coming along very well, Holly."

I look back over at the wall.

"Do you want to look?" she says gently.

I hesitate, then nod and look over as I try to swipe away the big hot tears rolling down my cheeks. She moves the wand around and stops and pushes a few buttons and then moves it again, and I stare as a baby comes into view. *Wow.*

I try to remember to breathe in and out as warmth fills me. She pushes more buttons, then reaches over and hands me a few pictures that she printed. I clutch them and watch the monitor in fascination with every stroke of the ultrasound paddle. A real baby is there.

"The baby's heartbeat is strong. Do you already know the gender?" she asks as she pushes the ultrasound Doppler deeper into my abdomen, and her face studies the monitor intently. The family received the results in an envelope at my twenty-four-week appointment. I thought the less I knew, the easier it would be to stay detached, and it was just the Coopers' baby. But now everything has changed in an instant.

"I didn't want to know." I shake my head.

"Do you want to know now?" she asks, her eyebrows slightly rising as she sees on the screen.

I suck in a breath through my teeth. "No, not yet. I think I want to be surprised. Honestly, I've had enough shocks to my system today. Let's save some for later."

She nods and chuckles. "Fair enough. What made you want to become a surrogate?"

"The couple had trouble conceiving, and I needed the money," I admit. It really was as simple as that. Only it's turning out to be anything but simple. We were helping each other.

"That's understandable, but I think it would be a good

idea to add to your support system. It might not be a bad thing to let a few trusted close people in on what you're doing," she says as she types a few things on the computer she has on wheels next to her.

I nod, guilt filling me, thinking my irresponsibility could be why I'm here right now, and I might have let everyone down. They're counting on me.

"SJ and I are available if you'd like to add us to your roster," she says softly, her hand covering mine.

"Thanks, Callie." This simple statement from her reminds me that I'm not alone, and I have people I can rely on and lean on. I feel silly for trying to do this on my own now.

"How much sleep are you getting?" she asks, wiping off my stomach with a towel and gently tugging my sweatshirt down.

"As much as I can. But I'm working a lot," I admit.

"This late in your pregnancy, you need to rest as much as possible. It sounds like you might be doing too much. It's not going to be good for you or the baby if you overdo it," she advises as she makes notes on my chart.

I run through my schedule and list and think about what I could trim and cancel, and honestly, I need the money now more than ever before this baby comes. Who knows what life will look like with a tiny human outside of my body relying on me now.

"Did you eat this morning?" she asks as she moves the

machine out of the way and looks at me.

"I grabbed a scone at the inn," I say sheepishly. Probably not the best choice.

She looks over at me, and her eyes shine. "Are you staying out at the Golden Gable Inn?"

"Yes, I'm staying in the studio apartment above Evan's garden shed," I say as I straighten my sweatshirt and sit up.

"The garden shed. That's where everybody stays for a time or two. It's beautiful since they remodeled it."

I nod. "It has been a great place to stay, and I'm grateful."

She looks at me and says firmly with her lips pressed in a line, "Sasha would never let you get away with eating like that if she knew you were pregnant. She also could be added to your support system roster. She's also good at keeping secrets."

She's not wrong. The chef at the inn, Sasha, is so kind to me and is a fantastic cook. I hate hiding this from the people I love and care about, but I have a plan. *Had a plan.*

"Who is your OB-GYN?" she asks as she listens to my heart with her stethoscope.

"I've been seeing a doctor and nurse at the surrogacy office for all my checkups. I'll probably have to find a new OB-GYN now since I'm not technically a surrogate anymore." I need to figure out what's going to happen to my medical care now, and I'm thankful I have a lawyer who will help me. If I have to pay for this myself, I'm screwed because I don't have health insurance at the moment working my part-time jobs.

She nods. "You have a lot to figure out, but you're not alone, Holly. If you need me to, I can get you an OB referral. Let us help you, okay?"

"Okay," I say softly with defeat. I know she's right. I'll need help now, and hiding this pregnancy is pointless because this baby will be here soon. With me. And I will have some explaining to do to everyone around me. Plus, my belly is becoming more and more obvious. I'm convinced a lot of people suspect but are just too nice to comment on whether I have gained weight or am carrying a watermelon under my shirt like Baby in *Dirty Dancing*.

"I think you're dehydrated and exhausted. If you keep up this pace, you might find yourself on bed rest for the remainder of your pregnancy. You need to keep your blood pressure down and get plenty of rest. And eat nutritious foods," she adds.

"I can't be on bed rest. I have to work," I say as I puff my cheeks and blow out a breath. I know things have to change, but I have no idea how I'll do all of it.

She holds my gaze. "But you have your own health and a baby to think about first."

A baby.

I hadn't let myself really envision the baby, let alone make a connection to it. It's just easier not to think about it and pretend it's a job. Less painful that way. I read books. Don't get attached, be professional, yada, yada. I'm doing my best.

But now the game has changed. It's not a game anymore. It's my life, and it's about to look a whole lot different.

"They're back," Dr. Reid murmurs as she pushes a button on her computer and pushes it toward the door. She squeezes my shoulder and reminds me, "I mean it, SJ and I are here if you need anything."

Hank and Ophelia step into the room, and Ophelia looks at Hank and back at me nervously.

"Thanks, Dr. Reid," I call out to her as she waves and heads out of the room.

"How's the baby?" Opi's biting her lip and glancing nervously at Hank, who is still here.

"Baby's fine," I say with a sigh of relief.

She swallows and looks at Hank. "Hank and I had a little chat in the cafeteria."

I smile as I try to sit up. "Oh yeah? That's great."

Hank leans against the doorway, and they exchange another look.

"What?" I ask skeptically as I look at them, realizing something is up with them.

"Okay, before you freak out..." Opi holds up a hand and grimaces slightly.

"Just tell me." I shake my head, sitting up. Not much can get worse today.

"Hank and his brother own Freedom Pie," she blurts out.

I frown. I was wrong. Things can get worse.

My mouth opens and closes. I don't know what to say, and Hank fills the void.

"So I hear you're the one who's been giving my brother a hard time," he says with a grin, that dimple popping again.

"Your brother," I stammer. "Your brother is running my family's restaurant into the ground," I huff as I lay my forearm over my face and groan in frustration.

"Well… we both are," he says nervously with a grin. "I'm more of a silent partner, but Beau is the one primarily running the business. Well, running it into the ground like you said, I guess. He needs help," he says, scrubbing a hand over his face and looking perplexed.

"I've repeatedly offered to buy it back for a fair price. He won't even respond to my offers." I look at Opi, who looks sympathetic and less like she's looking at Hank like a snack now.

Then guilt fills me when I look at Hank and his kind eyes. I think about how nice he's been to me today. If this is what one of the brothers is like, what if the other brother is just as pleasant? It was easier to hate the two curmudgeon older men I had pictured in my head. But not two younger guys; one of them out risking his own life putting out fires and rescuing sad, fragile, pregnant substitute teachers. I wonder what the other brother is like.

CHAPTER 4

Beau

"Did someone call the fire department?" Hank calls as he saunters into the kitchen during what was supposed to be our dinner rush, holding a stack of flat empty moving boxes under his arm and packing tape. He pauses and waves his hand at the smoky smell and looks at me skeptically.

I glance up at him impatiently and glare. "Very funny."

"Just teasing, grumpy butt," he says as he picks a piece of pizza off the cutting board and takes a bite, making a face as he chews.

I stand back and wait because I know what's coming.

"What did you do to that poor pizza?" he admonishes as he chews and struggles to swallow it, making a disgusted face.

"My best, Hank. I'm doing my best." I huff, my hands on my hips, and glare at him. "Are you here to pack up or give me a hard time?"

"The last time you let me cook, I *almost* started a fire. I think we've established that you're the cook in the family, not me," Hank says as he looks around.

"And I'd offer to help in the dining room, which I believe you told me is the only place I'm allowed to help from now on, but there are no customers. Is this normal for a Friday night?" he asks as he chucks the rest of the pizza into the trash and starts assembling what looks like a salad, adding piles of meat toppings.

"No, it's not," I mutter. I lean back on the counter and sigh. We should be busy with families filling the tables and eating and have a steady stream of takeout orders. I sent my waitstaff home twenty minutes ago because we haven't had a single customer since lunchtime, and even then, we only had a sprinkle of customers. Something's up, and whatever it is, it's not good.

"Face it, Beau, you need help. Someone who knows pizza and can make it like it was before we bought the place," he says, pointing his fork at me like he's just come up with a novel idea that hasn't already crossed my mind nearly a dozen times a day.

I roll my eyes and begin to clean up the kitchen for the

night. Stress cleaning helps me get through at this point.

Out of the corner of my eye, I swear I see something flash by on the ground, and my head whips around, but nothing is there. I swear to God, if we have rodents, that will be the final straw that'll make me lose my damn mind. "Did you see that?" I ask Hank.

"See what?" Hank mutters as he scrolls on his phone, not looking up.

"Never mind," I huff as I shut down the kitchen.

"You need a co-chef," Hank says as he tucks his phone back in his pocket.

"And where do you suppose I find a co-chef?" I mutter as I toss the pizza into the trash with the previous six I've ruined because I just can't get it right, no matter what I do. I wipe down the counter in frustration.

"I'm so glad you asked," Hank grins at me, "I know just the person."

"Who?" I grump.

"Holly Springs."

I narrow my eyes at him. "The previous owners' daughter?"

"That's the one. You need *her*," he says as he looks around, and his eyes settle on the trash full of failed pizza attempts that mock me daily.

"And why would you even remotely think that's a good idea? She wants to buy the place back from us. Her attorney 'Preston somebody' keeps sending me offer letters to buy us out. And we're not selling." I practically growl in frustration.

"Okay, I agree, not selling. But I think you could both help each other."

"What do you mean?" I sigh, wishing he would just cut to the chase and tell me what he means. "Between her offer letters and letters from the bank saying that we're dangerously close to getting behind, I'm in trouble. I don't know if we can afford help."

"I think you both could use each other's help. And she's sweet. I think you'd like her."

"What aren't you telling me?" I sigh.

He shrugs. "You just need to find her and talk to her. That's all I can say."

I close my eyes and lean my head back. I don't have time for this. I need help, not someone who wants to see my business fail so they can buy it out from under us. I have put everything I have into this restaurant, and so has Hank. I can't let him down.

Hank looks at his watch and back at me. "I gotta go pack up. I have plans tonight with some new friends. You need to get out of here too and meet people. Who knows, maybe they'll feel sorry for you and come eat here once they get to know you." He heads up the back stairs to our apartment above the shop. My apartment now that he's staying at his own place. While Hank drives me nuts sometimes, we needed our own places. He's an extrovert, loud and always making noise. I'm quieter, introverted, and like my solitude. I'll miss him, though. He and I are close, and he's the only family I have. I'm grateful for his help with the restaurant, even if I'm sending it spiraling down the toilet daily.

He's probably right. I've been hiding out here at the restaurant, and one thing I've discovered about small towns is that everyone is tight-knit, and if I don't start being friendly and going out to meet people, it'll probably hurt the business even more.

Hank stacks and tapes up boxes at the bottom of the stairs and asks, "Hey, have you met a guy named Stephen?"

I think for a minute and can't recall. "No, why?" I call back as I check on the dough I prepped for tomorrow, punching dough that's probably going to turn out just as disgusting as the last batch. It tastes like play dough, and I can't get the consistency right now, no matter how many different recipes I try.

Hank stacks up another load of boxes. "I don't know. People just keep asking how Stephen is doing." He shrugs. "Never met the guy."

"I don't know a Stephen," I say, but I still rack my brain trying to think. Although I've tried to remember the few customers that we have had.

"It's going to be okay, Beau." Hank looks at me with a mixture of pity and promise. "We'll get everything figured out."

Hearing Hank say this fills me with guilt, like a punch to the gut. As the older brother, I should be the one reassuring him. It's my job. I'm not supposed to be the one to mess things up. I'm the fixer.

I wish I had more of Hank's enthusiasm. He's always been a positive thinker and believed in whatever we're doing. Which I normally would, too. But right now? I honestly don't know if we'll make it here at Freedom Pie. I'm letting Hank down too, and I hate it. We both worked tirelessly and have poured our entire savings into this place. We moved here together because Hank wanted to join the fire department, and I wanted to open my own restaurant. We wanted to start over in the same place. And here I am, fucking it up for both of us. At least if we do end up having to sell Freedom Pie, he still has his job with the fire department. What would I have? Nothing. I'll be jobless, homeless, and have lost all of my savings that I sank into this place. Not to mention Hank's savings too. We both have skin in the game here at Freedom Pie.

I sigh with relief as a mobile order comes through for a pickup. I quickly pull the ingredients back out and get the pizza going, relieved to have something to do. I'm sliding it into the box when the bell on the front door dings, and a gentleman comes in and waves as he makes his way to the pickup window.

"Large pepperoni?" I call, and the guy nods as I ring him

up.

"Thanks." He taps his card on the machine. "Not too busy tonight?" He looks around at the deserted dining room.

I shake my head and try to sound casual when I ask, "Something going on in town tonight?"

He looks up, his expression sheepish, and says, "Black market pizza."

"What?" I blanch.

He scrubs a hand over his face. "There's a pizza pop-up shop down the street. Black market pizza."

I bet I know who's behind that. This has Holly Springs written all over it. I know it. That woman has been relentless in trying to buy her family's pizzeria back. I can't believe Hank even remotely thinks we should work with that woman. I don't get why she's even doing this. When Hank and I bought the business, her parents said nothing about their daughter's interest. In fact, they were in a rush to transfer ownership and quickly move out of state. They were an older couple, so I assume the daughter is probably in her forties or fifties. I've never met her, but I know she isn't a fan of us having the restaurant, judging by the persistent letters from her attorney repeatedly offering to buy us out. She's probably rejoicing at the prospect of our business failing, which makes me even more determined to succeed.

I've worked in the restaurant industry as a chef and owner for a few years now, and I didn't think running a pizza place would be this hard. However, it turns out that making pizza is not as easy as I thought it would be, and I can't get it right to save my life. It's like there's a spell on this place. My sauce tastes like garbage. My dough turns out awful. No matter what I do, it's all a mess. Ask me to cook a steak or any basic recipe, and I'll make it perfectly. Pizza, though? For the love of God, pizza is going to take me down. Pizza shouldn't be this hard.

"Thanks for coming in," I say as I slide his pizza and receipt over to the man.

"Thanks. Have a good night." He takes the pizza and waves as he heads out.

I watch him leave. Then curiosity gets the best of me when I think about this black-market pizza. What's he talking about? I slide on my coat and pull my hat low and head out back to take the trash out. I open the dumpster. "What the hell?"

The dumpster is full of my pizza boxes, and they are still full of pizzas. I throw my head back and groan. Word is probably getting around about how terrible my pizza tastes. That's why it's a ghost town here. I need to turn this around and do it fast. This is bad.

I walk around to the front of the building and look down both sides of the street. Baked Inn Love bakery is dark, but people appear from around the back carrying black pizza boxes.

What the hell?

I make my way down the street and watch as a line of people forms at the back door of the bakery.

People walk up to the back door and tap their card on a reader, and a black pizza box is handed to them through the doorway. I can't see the person in the doorway, just their hands.

I lean back against the building and cross my arms and watch. About a dozen people come and go quickly, same process repeated.

My blood boils with every customer that passes. I'm beyond frustrated and irritated to be undersold like this.

This person is stealing my business. They created a pop-up pizza shop out of the back of the bakery. I'm fuming. Who does this lady think she is? It must be that Holly Springs. I wonder if this evil middle-aged woman will have the horns, fangs, and spiked tail I envision. I get in line, curiosity getting the best of me to see for myself.

"Thanks, Holly, glad you're back," a customer calls with a wave as they head off with their black pizza box.

So it is her. I shake my head in disbelief at the confirmation.

I wait as she calls out, "Next."

I make no move and wait for her to step outside. And when she does, I'm shocked. She's nothing like I imagined. She's younger than I assumed and so beautiful I can't help but stare, taking her in. She's younger than me, late twenties if I had to guess. Her curly hair is pulled up on top of her head, and she's wearing an oversized white chef's jacket buttoned up to the neck.

"Do you have an order?" she calls out as her light hazel eyes land on mine. "Shit," she utters, her eyes widening.

"Shit," I repeat back, dryly.

"Are you Beau?" she asks as her eyes dart down the alley and back to me.

"I am." I cross my arms and stare at her lush pink lips. Her face is flushed from either the heat of the kitchen or her surprise reaction to seeing me catch her in the dirty act of her black market pizza.

"You look just like Hank," she concludes, her eyes sweeping over me as well.

"Hank looks like *me*. And *you* look like you're stealing my business," I counter, arms still crossed as I do my best to glare at her.

CHAPTER 5

Holly

What's the first rule of black market pizza?

We don't talk about black market pizza.

"Who talked?" I demand, placing my hands on my hips.

"Doesn't matter," he says, standing there with his arms crossed, looking like he's ready to duel with me over pizza. His body language pretty much says "give me a reason." And I get the passion. I'm passionate about pizza, too.

I wondered when I'd get to finally meet the other pizza brother. I figured I would eventually run into him at the inn or around town. I didn't think about what would happen if he showed up when I convinced Allie to let me borrow the bakery tonight to run my pop-up pizza shop. I have just been trying to make money since I'm not sure how much longer I can work and run these pop-ups before the baby comes.

We begin a short staring contest that he wins. I realize he's better looking than his brother, and I didn't think that was possible. Whatever is in the Sutton DNA is *good* stuff.

"I have to hand it to you. It's genius marketing," he admits, looking over at the stack of ominous black pizza boxes with no words, only a small squirrel in the bottom right corner of every box. I'm pretty proud of them myself.

"Thank you?" I say cautiously, looking at him guarded like he could potentially swipe them all and throw them all in the trash.

"Only one problem."

"What's that?" I counter.

"You're stealing from me."

"Excuse me?" I stand straighter. "I am a proprietor, just like you. No rule says we can't have more than one pizza place in this town."

"Maybe"—he shrugs—"but you know it's a dick move. I could turn you in."

"Turn me in? To who?" I laugh at his audacity. "I've committed no crimes."

"The health department," he continues. "Or someone."

I laugh. "Okay, go ahead and try."

"I'm sure I can come up with some crime to turn you in for," he hedges.

"The real crime is your pizza," I reply smugly. Last week, I paid a high school kid to secretly go and get me a pie from him, and that pizza was an abomination.

He says nothing, but his eyes narrow.

Frustration builds as he continues to glare at me, not saying a word, with his arms crossed and looking like a hot pizza menace.

"You took my business from *me*. Freedom Pie is *my* family's legacy, and I want it back. I've offered to buy it countless times for more than a fair price. And *you're* the dick for not even responding."

"You can't have it. It's *my* family legacy now." He glares.

Heat fills me in frustration. "Well, then you won't mind if we have a little friendly neighborhood competition for pizza, will you?" I tilt my head, challenging him.

"What kind of neighbor *are* you?" he asks. "Because a good neighbor wouldn't do this to another neighbor."

"The kind that makes better pizza than you." I smile sweetly.

A dark look crosses his face, but it's gone as quickly as it appears. He has a good poker face; I'll give him that. He says nothing but stares me down. He has the same beautiful eyes as Hank, only he's taller and built differently. More muscular and not as friendly. Hank has the personality of a golden retriever or a Dalmatian. Beau has the personality of a black cat or German shepherd. My breath hitches just looking at him.

What a waste of good looks on such a dick of a man.

"Sell it to me," I plead. "I'll double my last offer."

"I'll never give it up," he says firmly.

"I've heard about your pizza. Get out while you still can."

His eyes narrow. "Why are you like this?"

I narrow my eyes back. "Why are *you* like this?"

Before I can react, he reaches out with catlike reflexes and swipes a pizza box off the top of the stack. He opens it, takes a slice, and then a bite.

"Now who is stealing?" I purse my lips and wait for his reaction.

The smell of pizza fills the air as he chews while looking at me. "Fuck, that *is* good." He glares, and his shoulders sag with defeat.

I put my hands on my hips. "I've been making pizza for over twenty years."

"What were you, like five?" he asks as he still glares at me while he chews.

I say nothing, mesmerized as I watch his reaction as he eats the pizza I've poured love into for this town. I'm not good at much, but pizza is in *my* DNA. It's what I know and what I love. To me, it's more than just a business. It's my passion to feed people and be a part of our community. I miss it so much.

He swallows the pizza, his eyes still on me. But I can see

it in his eyes that he's thinking and trying to figure out my pizza recipe by taste. He'll never figure it out. It's a secret family recipe we've made for over forty years. I had to learn it by watching my parents make it daily for years.

"Can't figure it out, can you?" I laugh a little, casually baiting him. I know I shouldn't, but I can't resist.

Dammit, why does he have to be so good looking?

He looks at me, tucks the pizza box under his arm, and calls over his shoulder as he strolls away, "See you around, Polly."

"It's Holly," I huff, glaring at his retreating back. "And you didn't pay for that!"

I watch as he walks away, admiring his back, reminding myself that he's still the enemy. And he stole my pizza. I clean up the shop quickly because I promised Allie that I would. I told her she'd never even know I was there. Not a crumb left in her kitchen. Tonight was a smashing success, and I want to make sure she'll still allow me to do it, even if it pisses off Beau. I have a baby to raise now. Maybe I could even get a food truck. I do a final sweep of the kitchen, making sure to leave it perfect. I try to picture myself doing these pop-up shops with a baby, and I realize maybe I can make this work for now.

Sure, I could just open my own pizza shop, but I want *my* shop back. Call me nostalgic, but I want the oven I first learned to bake in and the apartment full of memories. I could start over, but it wouldn't be the same. I want Freedom Pie back. All my core memories are there, and I want to continue these memories and traditions with my own family someday. I close my eyes when I remind myself that someday is really soon.

I wonder if I'm even qualified to be a mother. I'm pretty sure I'm not even fit to be a pet owner. But I have a visceral feeling inside me that this baby needs to stay with me now and be loved and cherished. He or she doesn't deserve the hand dealt here. I'll do my best to be the best mom I need to be. Suddenly, I feel like I need to buckle down even more to get Freedom Pie back. Beau may not be ready to sell today, but tomorrow is another day. I'll keep saving and waiting.

I lock up and walk down Main Street, carrying the last pizza box with me. I collapse onto a bench across the street from Freedom Pie and stare at it. The front windows are dark, and the apartment above it is lit up. I haven't walked by the front of it for a while now. The last time I walked by, it still smelled like home, and I almost couldn't bear it so I've steered clear of it. I miss Stephen, too. I wonder who is taking care of him.

"Hey, Holly, how are you doing?" I glance up and see Hank coming out of Freedom Pie carrying an armful of boxes, smiling as he strolls toward me.

Feeling guilty that I've been scheming to get my shop back from him, I say, "I'm good. How are you?"

"I'm great but more concerned about you. How have you been feeling?" he asks as he looks at me, setting his boxes down and plopping beside me on the bench.

"I'm hanging in there," I admit. "I also just met your brother."

He chuckles. "Oh yeah? How did that go?"

"He busted my black market pizza ring." I sigh. "It didn't go well."

Hank throws his head back and laughs as he looks over at me. "I bet you'd like him if you got to know him."

I scoff. "I wouldn't bet on that. How is it you two share the same DNA?"

He shrugs. "He's just having a hard time with the pizza place. It's his dream, too, you know. He really wants this to work."

I never thought of it that way. As I was mourning the loss of it all, I never thought about it being someone else's dream. We're fighting for the same thing.

"You know," Hank says. "You two could do this together."

"Do what together?" I look at him skeptically.

"You could both run Freedom Pie."

I look at him as if he's lost his mind. "Why would I do that? I can open my own restaurant."

"You could. Or you could have a partner to share the workload with so you can have plenty of time for your baby." He shrugs.

I wouldn't hate that. But with Beau? He makes abominable pizza. And he's rude. And really cute. Ugh.

"I'm just saying. There are ways to make this work. You both could help each other." Hank shrugs.

"Want some pizza?" I say with defeat, nodding to the last pizza next to me that I notice he's staring longingly at.

He laughs. "Is that even a question?"

I open the box, and he takes a slice. He takes a bite and moans and looks over at me. "That is *so* good. What do you put in this? You need to teach Beau."

I snort a laugh. "I'm not teaching him. He's my competition."

"He's not your competition, but he could be your partner," he says thoughtfully as he chews his bite.

"I talked to him about you earlier," he continues as he looks at me thoughtfully and takes another bite.

My eyes cut to him, and he holds up his hands. "About helping out with the pizza place, nothing else."

I didn't figure he would tell anyone about the other day at the school, but relief fills me that my secret is still safe. "Why would you think I would want to partner with him? I want to buy it back."

"Hear me out," he says. "What if you bought *me* out? What if *you* partnered with Beau?"

Interesting. "I don't know…"

"What if you could quit all your random jobs and do what

you truly love, which is running Freedom Pie again? You might not be the sole owner, but you could even scale back and have one job instead of four or five? Or even half a job since you'd have Beau as a partner."

"I don't know," I admit. "We didn't exactly start off on the right foot."

"I think you guys would be fine once you get to know him." He shrugs.

"Is your brother moving?" I ask him, suddenly realizing he's got a load of moving boxes. "Satan is probably preparing your brother's new bedroom as we speak."

"Moving out," he says proudly and laughs. "I got my own place, so now Beau and I have our own bachelor pads," he says as he nods to the top of Freedom Pie.

"He's single?" I ask, looking back up at the building. "Gee, I wonder why."

"He is now. He's been through a lot. Sounds like you both have. You have more in common than you think." He stretches his long legs out in front of him and looks up at the apartment.

The more I learn about these brothers, the harder I find it to dislike them.

Sadness fills me when I picture someone else living in my family home. It feels wrong.

"I have an idea." He looks over at me. "What are you doing tonight?"

I shrug. "Heading home to the inn, why?"

"Why don't you stop by McGuiness Tavern tonight? I was hoping to see Ophelia there. Maybe you could help me convince her to come. It would be nice to have a wing lady," he says with a smile.

"You do not seem like the type of guy who needs a wing lady," I say dryly.

"It's hard being the new guy," he pleads. "Plus, we can go hang out with everyone."

"I don't really hang out anymore," I admit. Lately, I've been good at hiding in the garden shed at the inn or staying busy with as many jobs as possible. My friends and I have basically been texting to keep up, and I opt out of most social events. They're starting to notice more and say something so I probably should show up to something.

"All the more reason to get out of the house and have a little fun," he says matter-of-factly, and his dimple pops. One that I noticed that Beau has as well.

"Fine, I guess I can." I reach into my pocket for my phone. "I'll send Opi a text."

"Yes!" Hank does a fist pump and takes another bite of pizza.

Me: Want to go to McGuiness tonight? Your excited Dalmatian Hank's coming and wants you to come too.

Opi: Are you serious? What time?

Me: Here in a bit. I need to run home and shower first.

Opi: I'll pick you up in about an hour. Tell me everything. I'm finishing a poodle grooming.

Me: Thanks!

"Well, you've got yourself a date. She's picking me up, and we'll be there in an hour," I say as I slide my phone into my pocket.

He's just finished his slice of pizza and eyes my pizza box again.

"Want the rest of this?" I say as I lift the lid to tempt him.

"Absolutely." He takes the pizza box and immediately goes for another slice.

"Hey, have you seen Stephen?" I ask curiously. "I haven't been able to check in on him, and I'm worried about how he's doing."

Hank looks confused. "Who *is* Stephen?"

My eyes widen, and I stand. "You haven't been taking care of him?"

"I don't even know the guy," he says, closing the box with alarm and standing, too.

"Come on, I'll introduce you two." I sigh as we walk around the building and up to the back porch of Freedom Pie. I stand on the railing and look up and over the top of the porch roof where his little gazebo house is positioned out of sight, so he has his privacy. My dad and I built and painted it for Stephen a few years ago. It could probably use a fresh coat of paint now.

"Stephen," I call, worried.

He pokes his little squirrel head out of his house, looking sleepy.

"Hey, buddy," I coo. I motion for Hank to come closer. "This is Hank."

Stephen shoves his plump furry body through his swinging doors and comes to the edge of the roof, inspecting us to see if we've brought him any food.

"Let him have a piece of your crust, please," I tell Hank. There's no telling where he's been getting his food. I should have been checking on him. Guilt fills me when I think about him hungry out here in the cold.

He rips a piece off and hands it to Stephen, who greedily gobbles it with his little hands. He eyes Hank suspiciously but doesn't seem to mind him.

"I've missed you," I murmur sadly.

"I don't think Beau has a clue about him," Hank says in awe as he hands him another piece of crust. "I didn't know the restaurant came with a squirrel."

"He doesn't bother anyone, and local people know him. My dad always gave him fruit, nuts, and vegetables. I should start bringing him food. I just assumed you guys would take care of him."

"You just assumed we knew and would feed the resident pet squirrel?" Hank looks at me and laughs. "People kept asking me how he was. I thought he was a human I hadn't met yet."

I snort as I laugh. "Well, when you put it that way."

Hank reaches over and scratches his body, Stephen leaning into him. "He's pretty cool."

"Leaving this place has been hard, and I miss him," I admit.

"Do me a favor?" Hank asks with a grin.

"What?" I look at him dryly.

"Don't tell Beau about Stephen just yet. Let's mess with him," he says. "I think he thinks there's a rodent loose in the restaurant."

"Okay, just please don't let anything happen to him. He's a good little friend," I say softly.

"I won't." Hank's mouth turns up in a sad smile. "I'm sorry, Holly. We had no idea about you and thought we were the only offer your parents were considering."

I watch as Stephen retreats into his house when he realizes we have nothing else for him. "If it wasn't you guys, it would have been someone else."

"We can get you and Beau in a better place, and then maybe you can consider my idea. I think it could benefit both of you."

"I don't know...I have so much going on right now," I lament. I don't have time for Beau and his grumpy attitude.

"Which is exactly why you don't have to consider anything but having fun for tonight. Let's head out and have some fun, wing lady," he says as he heads back and scoops up his boxes and loads them into his truck.

Once he's finished, he calls over to me, "You need a ride?"

"No, I have my car in front of the bakery." I nod. "Just taking a break before I head out."

"See you at the tavern, wing lady," he calls, waving as he drives off.

I reluctantly look back at the only place that's ever truly felt like home. Sitting out here on this bench is as close as I'll ever get to it now.

Since I moved to the inn, I'll admit, it's been lonely. Despite Beth and Evan making me feel comfortable, I've struggled to find my new identity now that I'm starting over. Allie has let me use the bakery for my pop-up shop. And Paige has given me a job at the bookstore. At a time in my life when I felt like I lost everything, this town pulled me in and showed me love.

What if I *could* get it back in some way? It might be worth putting up with Beau to at least get part of my dream back.

Beth: Sasha reminded me that you had a pop-up tonight. How did it go, Holly?

Me: Really great! Sold out in two hours. Met the other pizza brother.

Paige: Uh-oh, how did that go?

Me: Not good. He isn't a fan of his competition. (Devil smiling emoji)

Mellie: He's so hot, though. Both of the pizza brothers are. I've seen them but have not officially met them.

Me: I've met both. Not a fan of the grumpy one.

Beth: Holly, are you coming to McGuiness tonight? Evan is playing with the band. We're meeting up at nine to have appetizers and drinks.

Allie: I'm here with Evan warming up now. Please come, Holly!

Me: I'm coming! Ophelia is picking me up.

Beth: Oh, nice! I'll see you there. Just getting the babies down for Margie to babysit. Who else is coming?

Mellie: I'm in. Paige, want to go?

Paige: Yes! I can pick you up on the way, Mel.

Callie: I just got off shift. SJ and I will meet you there.

CHAPTER 6

Beau

"What's in your hand?" I demand as Hank stands in the kitchen with his hand frozen holding a slice of pizza over the black pizza box open on the counter.

"Pizza," Hank says with a mouthful of pizza, looking guilty. He swallows, then his mouth turns up in a wide grin. "What's that in *your* hand?"

"Research," I say, dropping the traitor pizza on the counter and folding my arms across my chest. "We need to talk about Holly."

"It's delicious research," he says as he pops a piece of pepperoni in his mouth.

"You do realize that if this place fails, you lose money, too, right?" I remind him.

"This is why I've been telling you that you need her help. She can help us. She loves this place, man. It was her family's. She doesn't want it to fail." He closes the pizza box and tilts his head expectantly to me.

"She does want us to fail. She pretty much told me that tonight. I can figure this out. This is *our* family business," I hedge.

"Beau, look at this place. It's a sinking ship. The bank is sending us letters. You're being stubborn, and we've barely had any customers all week."

I scrub a hand down my face. "I know." I don't want to admit it, but I'm in over my head.

"Come out with me tonight to McGuiness Tavern. A bunch of the locals are going, and it'll be good for you to mingle with them."

"I can't. I have a bunch of things to do." I pull in a breath and let it out.

"Like what?" he challenges.

"This place is a mess. I have cleaning to do. Food to prep." I lament, raising my chin, hoping he'll leave me alone and get off my back.

He gives me a knowing look. "This place is spotless. You've probably already stress-cleaned it several times today, and you have no customers, so no food needs prepped," he says as he gives me a look. This might have worked on someone else but not on my brother. He knows me too well.

"Fine, I'll go." I sigh with defeat. "I guess it can't hurt."

"Good. Stop being such a little pissy pants," he says, grabbing a soda from the cooler.

I roll my eyes and let that comment slide. "How're the renovations coming along?" I ask, changing the subject.

Hank bought a small older house on the edge of town and has been slowly fixing it up. We've worked on it together and made it livable, but he still has his work cut out for him.

"Good. Getting ready to gut one of the bathrooms next." He takes a swig of his soda.

"Let me know when you need my help," I offer.

"I'll take any help I can get. You ready to head out?" he says as he picks up his pizza box and heads to the door.

"Sure," I grump, sliding my ball cap back on.

"And do me a favor? Don't be a party pooper. No one wants to be around a wet blanket," he calls as I playfully punch him in the shoulder and lock the door.

"Oh, and I met Stephen. You're going to love the guy," he calls before he shuts the door to his truck.

"The pizza brothers are here!" someone calls out as we step into McGuiness Tavern, and Hank nudges me. "Lose the scowl, man. At least try not to look like a menace."

"Hmph," I mutter as I look around and take in the tavern with the natural wood walls. A band plays at the front, and nearly all the tables are filled with patrons buzzing with chatter, laughter heard from across the room, and sounds of dishware clinking. This is what I dreamed of when I bought Freedom Pie. A place where people would gather, have good food, and make memories. I wanted a place full of laughter and fun.

I follow Hank to a table full of younger people about our age, and I recognize a few familiar faces from around town. We're greeted with smiles from everyone at the table except for one person. Holly. She's sitting along the wall, her head down, studying her menu as if her life depends on it. Her body language isn't happy like the others at the table. And I don't miss the way she glances up at me and quickly back down to the menu.

"Hank and Beau, glad you could make it," Beth says. "Everyone, meet the pizza brothers." I look over, and Holly is looking at me. Her expression looks pained hearing that. I close my eyes for a few seconds and take a deep breath. I hate that look on her face. I think she believes us to be archenemies, and maybe I thought so too, but then Hank shared his genius business idea. I don't know what it is about her, but her contradiction of steely determination and fragility has intrigued me.

Hank sits, and the only seat open is next to Holly. I

cautiously slide in next to her, careful to give her plenty of space. Suddenly, it feels warm in here, and I realize I'm nervous.

"Everyone introduce yourselves to Hank and Beau," Beth tells the table over the chatter and noise of the tavern.

A redhead with bright blue glasses smiles at me. "I'm Paige, and this is my fiancé, Preston. We own the Turn the Paige bookstore, and Preston is a lawyer in town," she says as she leans over to shake our hands. Preston shakes my hand and gives me a genuinely friendly smile. *Holly's lawyer.* Nice to put a face to the name. He looks like a nice guy. Can't fault the guy. He was just doing his job sending the letters.

A guy in a button-down shirt leans over and offers a hand. "I'm Logan, and my wife Allie is up singing with her brother Evan." He nods toward the band. We own the bakery in town, and I'm Beth's literary agent.

"And I'm Beth," the blonde with glasses reminds me with a grin. "And you know Evan, he's up there singing. We've been in a few times at Freedom Pie."

I nod to her. "Good to see you again."

Another blond woman leans over and shakes my hand. "I'm Mellie, and that is my fiancé, Ty. Ty works at the auto shop, and I'm the housekeeper at the inn," she says as she points at a man in a blue flannel shirt with a backward cap on down the table who waves and smiles as he chats with someone else at the table.

Another guy leans forward and says. "I'm SJ, and this is my wife, Callie. She's an emergency room physician, and I also work at Sam's Auto Shop and coach football up at the school." He reaches over to shake my hand firmly. He has a military look about him. I'll have to ask him about that later. I can usually spot another veteran in the crowd.

They seem like good people, and I won't admit it to Hank, but he was right, I'm glad I came out and met them.

I turn my head to Holly, meeting her worried gaze before she quickly looks away again. She fidgets in her seat like she's nervous.

These people have a good friendship, and they clearly love Holly. She's not the enemy I constructed in my head who wants me to fail here. No, they're all including me. And Hank. Inviting us into their friend group here. Hank was right; we need this. Not just for our business to succeed but it would also be nice to make some good friends here. It sucks being the new guy. Maybe I need to put down my sword and start over with Holly. We've gotten off on the wrong foot, and it's time for a do-over.

I look at her with new clarity I didn't have before, make eye contact, and say quietly, "Hi, I'm Beau. Maybe we can start over." I clear my throat softly and offer my hand out. I give her a smile and see one touch her lips as well. Her hand twitches hesitantly on the table like she's considering me for a moment.

"I'm Holly," she says as our hands meet, my thumb instinctively stroking across her knuckles. A move that feels more intimate than I intended. But when I look at Holly to gauge her reaction, she seems just as affected as I am. Her eyes dilate, a small gasp leaving her mouth, drowned out by the noise of the tavern but one that I feel all the same. My hand engulfs her much smaller but strong hand that grips mine. Her palm mirrors the woman before me, a contrast of mostly soft and smooth skin, but with a hint of roughness. Strong but supple.

"It's nice to meet you," I say, my hand still holding hers. I finally release her, but she doesn't pull back and keeps her hand tucked in mine for slightly longer, looking at me as entranced as I'm looking at her.

She looks nervous, and her eyes cut to me and back to the group a few times, like she's not sure what just happened between us.

"So what's good here?" I ask, trying to lighten the mood.

She slides over her menu and says, "They have great house beers and nachos."

"Is that what you're having?" I ask as I look over the menu.

"I'm having nachos . . . and a water," she adds nervously.

Hank joins in and pulls up a chair beside Ophelia across from us. "Hey, Holly, how was business tonight?" she asks cheerfully, then her face freezes when she looks over at me, panicking.

"He already knows about the black market pizza," Holly says dryly. "He even *likes* it."

"We're calling a truce," I declare, looking at Holly and back at the menu.

She shrugs. "Fine." But the look she gives me is anything other than fine. I have to figure out how to make her not hate me and sabotage me by the end of the night, or this will not go well.

We place our dinner orders and idly chat about food and music. Callie looks over and smiles. "So Beau and Hank, what made you guys land in Freedom Valley?"

Hank swipes a nacho chip and says, "I think we both wanted a fresh start, and when we found Freedom Pie, we knew it would be a good place for us to start over."

"What did you guys do before Freedom Pie?" Beth asks curiously. "Have you always been in the pizza business?"

Hank laughs. "I'm not really into the pizza business. I'm more of a silent partner. I'm a firefighter and a paramedic. Beau is the pizza guy. He used to be in the Army, and then he had another restaurant…" He grunts as I kick him under the table. I don't feel like talking about myself tonight, especially not the restaurant from before.

A guy who I vaguely recognize who was just performing in the band scoots in next to Beth. "What'd I miss?" he asks.

"Hi, honey," Beth says, leaning in to kiss him. "Evan, this is Beau and his brother, Hank. They own Freedom Pie now."

Evan nods curiously as he looks at Hank, me, and over at Holly. "Is that right?" he says, extending his hand. "Good to meet you both. Beth and I own the Golden Gable Inn. If you guys ever need anything, just let us know."

"Thanks, we appreciate that," I say as I take a pull of my beer. "Same to you." These people do seem nice.

"What did you do in the Army, Beau?" Callie asks as she nods to her husband. "SJ was in the Army, too."

"I was a cook," I say as I take a pull of my beer. Hank coughs into his fist, and I watch as SJ eyes me in disbelief. He chuckles and then takes a sip of his beer. Yeah, he's not buying it. And Hank's reaction didn't help. I frown at him. I need to talk with him about not telling everyone about my business.

"A cook? Huh." SJ gives me a small smile in disbelief. "That's what the Special Forces guys said when asked about their job. That or a supply clerk. And you, my friend, were probably neither," he says with a smile. He tips his beer at me, calling me out.

Hank laughs, and this is when I know he will totally out me here. "He absolutely was not a cook. What cook do you know speaks like three languages and is built like that?" He nudges me, and I cut my eyes to him and frown. But I can't be mad at Hank. I know he's proud of me. I'm just not as good at opening up to people as he is. And it was only two languages, not three. But I don't say that. I don't talk about that part of my life. It's just over. When Hank said we wanted a fresh start, he wasn't wrong. I wanted to start over here and make a new life and a future. That future doesn't include the Army anymore.

"Fine, I wasn't a cook *in* the military. But I was before, during, and after my time in the military," I say casually as I lean in and grab a nacho. I look over, and Holly is watching me curiously.

"Why'd you get out?" SJ asks as he snags his own chip.

I shrug. "Needed to be near family," I say, nodding to Hank. "Did my time. Why'd you get out?" I ask, turning the conversation onto SJ and off me. I can tell he notices what I'm doing and gives me a little nod and goes with it.

"A shoulder injury took me out a little earlier than planned. But I'm glad to be back here in Freedom Valley," he says as he leans back and puts his arm around a blue-eyed blonde who looks at him adoringly.

I envy the guy. I played the field in the military, and I'm not at that stage anymore. I'm not looking for casual dating, and I'm not looking to hook up with someone. When I moved to Freedom Valley, I decided to try to find someone who wanted to build a life with me, settle down, and wanted a family like me. I want someone to look at me like I hung the moon. Someday.

Luckily, the conversation turns to other people and not to me. Hank is having fun and was right. We needed this. He's in his element, laughing and making friends, and he makes it look so easy.

Holly drank two waters and ate nachos with the table. I noticed she's quiet and reflexively holds her stomach protectively at times. I wonder if she's just quiet around me or in general. Something tells me that she's not usually this quiet.

"So are you going to continue with your black market pizza?" I ask casually, sipping my beer.

She surprises me by saying, "Are you going to sell me the restaurant?" She says it with a smile like she's half joking.

This woman.

"Nope," I say with a pop of the p as I lean back and peel the label on my bottle and sneak looks at her when I think she's not looking.

"Then, I guess you'll just have to get used to the competition." She shrugs but gives me a look, and her mouth turns up slightly.

"I thought we were calling a truce?" I frown and tilt my head.

"We can call a truce and both be pizza shop owners," she offers with a smug smile.

"I'm sorry about the shop being sold. I didn't know there were other interested buyers," I say quietly.

She lets out a defeated sigh. "Just like I told Hank, it would have been someone else if it wasn't you."

But some unspecified part of me is glad that it was Hank

and me because something tells me that the more time that I spend with this enigmatic woman next to me, the more I'll want to know all there is to know about her.

CHAPTER 7

Beau

"I have a business proposition for both of you," Evan says as he looks over at Holly and me.

"Both of us?" Holly asks, confused, looking at me and back at Evan.

The table has quieted down, and Beth slides onto the bench next to Evan and leans into him.

"We're in a bind, guys," Beth says, looking perplexed.

"Our catering company just fell through for our wedding. We were thinking about just making the food ourselves, but we want to be able to enjoy our wedding. We need a caterer fast. We love Freedom Pie, and we were thinking of having a pasta bar, pizza, and breadsticks," Evan says, looking hopefully at me.

I straighten in my seat; this could be good. I'd love the business. But what does Holly have to do with this?

Luckily for me, Holly asks, "What do you mean about us both?"

Beth and Evan share a look.

"It's a big job," Beth says apologetically. "We figured maybe Holly could help you."

"I already have help at the restaurant," I start to say, and Evan interjects.

"Okay, I'm going to lay it out there, man," Evan says quietly. "We are really excited for you to have your new restaurant, and we want to support you. But we really miss the OG Freedom Pie pizza. Like bad. I'm sorry, but it just hasn't been the same. We were hoping you could do it together and Holly could help you? Even just for the wedding? We can pay you extra for the late notice."

"What Evan is trying to say," Beth interrupts, shooting Evan a warning look. "What if Holly helps you with your recipes and you were able to make the Freedom Pie pizza and pastas like we used to have?"

I can tell they're both trying to be nice. My pizza sucks. I'm not going to lie; it hurts to hear this. But we all know it's the truth. Yet they're still trying to give me a chance and help me. And for that, I'm grateful.

Hank leans over and whispers, "Do it. I told you that you

need to work with Holly."

Holly says nothing, but she looks lost in thought, and I wonder what she thinks about all of this. I do need help. But not help from someone who wants my business to fail so she can buy me out.

I really want to trust her, but I'm not sure how to after I've been down a similar path with another woman. I feel like a fool for letting my ex-wife play me like she did. It didn't end well for me.

"What do you think, Holly?" Evan asks her. *Shit.* If I don't agree with it, maybe they'll just hire her instead.

"I'll help," she says softly.

"You will?" I turn to her, shocked.

She looks at me and seems amused by my stunned reaction. Her eyes seem a little brighter and hopeful. "Beau and I can work out the details. But we'll make your day special for you. It's not a problem."

My eyes lock on Holly's, and I tilt my head to the entryway of the restaurant. "Can I talk to you for a second?"

I watch as she stands gingerly from her seat, her teeth nibbling that full bottom lip with nervousness, and smoothing her hands down a dark-colored baggy sweater that seems to dwarf her. A sweater that has me wondering what kind of curves she's hiding underneath.

I gently take her elbow to guide her out of the busy shoulder-to-shoulder tavern and into the entrance alcove.

I move closer to her so we can hear each other, and it ends up being so close that I can smell the hint of spices in her hair from making pizzas, but underneath is a hint of perfume and shampoo. A tantalizing aroma to me. "Are you sure you want to do this?"

"I said I was." She folds her arms, challenging me.

"Why would you want to help me?" I cross my arms and evaluate her intentions.

She lifts her chin defiantly. "I need the money."

"Even if it means working with me?" I question, still unsure of her objective.

She rolls her eyes. "I thought you called a truce."

"I thought *we* called a truce. But I'm making sure you are fully on board with that truce." I counter carefully, watching her reaction to see if she's messing with me or not.

She blows out a breath. "I need a job for some upcoming bills."

I nod uneasily. "Okay, we'll do it. Split everything halfway after the cost of supplies?"

She shrugs. "Sounds fair."

"And...you'll help me make the pizza like it was before?" I ask, suddenly feeling vulnerable.

A small smile spreads on her face. "You definitely need help with the pizza. I've had your pizza. It's still a crime."

"That's harsh." I cringe.

"Is it?" Her voice rises a few octaves, and she tilts her head in question.

I huff. "Fine, it's awful. I would appreciate your help with the pizza. But I thought you viewed me as your competition."

She twists her lips for a minute. "Hank said something to me earlier that was an interesting idea."

"What's that?" I counter.

"He mentioned maybe I could work with you. As a partner," she adds.

I watch her face to see if she has any ill intentions. She looks excited. Hopeful.

"Why would you even want to partner with me?" I ask, surprised that she would even be interested in that.

She shuffles her feet, resting her hands in front of her. "I miss the wood-fired oven in which my dad and I made countless pizzas. I miss the smell that permeates the air there, even the apartment above, making everything smell delicious. I miss the cracked vinyl on the seats in the dining room. I miss everything. It was home."

My face softens upon hearing this. "It seems that this town misses you at Freedom Pie, too."

She nods. "It might be good. I need the job. You need help. Hank might be right."

"Hank might be right," I echo with a nod.

"We could do a trial period. Just try out this catering job and this next week and see if we don't kill each other in the meantime." She looks at me, her eyes full of hope and something else I can't quite place.

"A trial period sounds good." I agree.

She nods, and for some reason, she seems to find it difficult to meet my eyes, her cheeks darkening. She's nervous.

The determination pulses through me to make her feel at ease. I'm also relieved she's willing to try.

She shuffles nervously as I step toward her. I extend my hand and say, "One week trial period and then we can decide if it's a good fit."

"Deal," she says as she slides her smooth and soft hand in mine, and I feel the pulse of my blood when her hand touches me.

This will be interesting.

"You promise not to kill each other?" Hank jokes as he looks back and forth between us when we sit back down at the table together.

I glare at him with my best menacing brotherly glare.

"No promises," Holly says with a laugh.

Evan looks relieved at Beth. "We still have a wedding."

"We still have a wedding," she repeats and kisses him.

She turns to us and gives us a look of relief. "Finally. We've been trying to get married for over a year, and life keeps happening."

"You really want pizza for your wedding?" Holly asks incredulously. "I could make something else. Maybe something a little more fancy."

"*We* could make something else." I clear my throat as I chime in, reminding her we're doing this together.

"Nope," Beth and Evan say quickly at the same time.

"We both love Freedom Pie very much, and I think we speak for this whole town when we say we miss it. No offense," Evan says, looking sheepishly at me. "If it takes our wedding to get it back to tasting the way it was, we volunteer our wedding as tribute."

"We'll work out the details," I add.

"Awesome!" Beth says. "I'll let everyone know. We've been so worried about how we're going to feed everyone. You guys are a lifesaver. I'm so grateful for you both."

"When's the wedding?" I ask, thinking we probably have several weeks to plan.

"In a week," Holly says.

"A week?" I choke.

"Is that a problem?" Evan asks, looking back and forth between us.

"Nope," I interject, holding up a hand. "We'll be ready."

What have I gotten myself into? *It's just pizza*, I remind myself. Just pizza.

CHAPTER 8

Holly

It's freezing outside. Winters in the Northeast are no joke, and this one is predicted to be the coldest winter in over a hundred years or something. Every time I step outside, I practically tiptoe so I don't slip on ice. I take my time driving to work, and my car struggles on the snow-packed roads. The plows are out, but I've heard they're having a hard time keeping up.

I pat my belly. "We'll get there safe, little pepper," I say. I still refuse to refer to the baby as an it. I thought little pepperoni was cute, pepper for short. Still getting used to the baby, and I will admit it's terrifying and exciting.

When I pull up to Freedom Pie, it feels good to be back,

yet somehow foreign. Like I don't belong in the place that was always home up until this year. It's a bittersweet feeling. I brush my feelings aside, and I get out of my car and check on Stephen. He's not in his little house, so he must be off doing whatever it is that squirrels do. I slide the baggy of nuts and dried fruit back into my pocket for later and climb down the railing.

"What're you doing up there?" Beau calls out of the cracked back door. He stands in the doorway, wiping his hands on a towel as I balance on the railing to peer up at Stephen's hideaway.

I look over and realize the back door is propped open, and it's freezing outside. I think back to my dad always making sure we shut the door. I close my eyes for a second at a quick memory of him teasing whoever left it open. I can almost feel my dad here, and the nostalgic memory of it springs a few hot tears to my eyes when I remember that this is Beau's restaurant now and my dad will never be here cooking with me again. I'll never have another memory here with my parents at the restaurant.

"Why is the door open?" I bark. "You're letting all the heat out." I realize that came out a little more aggressive than I meant for it to be. Jeez. I didn't want to start out on the wrong foot with Beau.

Beau clears his throat and looks back toward the kitchen. "I, um, was airing it out."

I pull off my scarf and hat and hang them on the hook out of habit, which is still next to the back door, and cough, waving away the burnt smell with my hand. "What did you burn?"

He runs his hands through his hair in frustration until both his hands are clasped together at the back of his head. His brow furrows as a look of defeat covers his face. "Everything. Listen, I'm a really good cook. I am. You probably don't believe me, but it's true. But it's like I'm cursed here. Nothing turns out right. I can't make even a basic pizza to save my life. Even my sauce is terrible." He looks so defeated and like he needs a hug.

I do feel sorry for him because I know how much I love cooking here, and if my food came out that way, I'd be devastated, too.

My thoughts drift back to what it would feel like to hug him, have him wrap his arms around me and hug me back. I wonder what he smells like, and if he's a good hugger. Maybe these pregnancy hormones are making me weepy and touchy-feely. Or maybe it's just that Beau is being vulnerable right now, and it's hot as hell.

Nope, I have to focus. I'm here to do a job, and that's it. I will keep telling myself that. We have a catering job to complete together, and I have to put my game face on for this. It's hard enough as it is coming back here.

I look around and take in everything. Very clean, spotless,

in fact. My parents would love it. Damn, it feels so weird being back here without them. A charred and black pizza is on the counter, which looks like the culprit of the horrible smell permeating the kitchen. I head over to the oven and immediately see what's going on. I reach behind it and turn a few buttons and adjust the knob on the front to where it needs to be.

"Why aren't you using the wood-fired oven?" I ask, confused as I look over at him watching me with a look of fascination on his face.

He heaves a deep sigh. "I can't get that going either. I've just been using the regular oven, but that's also not working right. I've only worked with newer appliances. This one is old."

"It isn't broken. I just adjusted it. You had a couple of buttons switched for broil and bake. It's an old oven, and it's just temperamental, but it's good to go now." No wonder his pizza always burns.

"I didn't even think of that. I googled it but came up with nothing."

"It's just old, but it works fine. It's a solid appliance. But we rarely used it for the pizza. Only for baking desserts and stuff."

I've missed using the wood-fired oven for pizza. My pop-up pizza has been just okay with Allie's baking ovens. The wood fire would have made all the difference, and I can't believe he hasn't been using it.

He nods like he's absorbing everything I'm telling him.

"Come on, I'll help you get the wood-fired oven going. Pizza in it and in the regular oven are two completely different experiences." I look around at the kitchen, feeling slightly more at home. I can't wait to sink my hands in the dough and create a pizza. I've missed this kitchen.

He pushes off the counter and follows me, relieved I'm here. "Thank you again for your assistance."

"Didn't my parents show you things and help you?" I say as I turn to him. I would think they would have shown him things, at least getting started. Then again, they weren't here as much toward the end and were at their condo in Florida, and I was content to run things on my own. Which shocked me. They didn't give me more time and abruptly shut the restaurant down when they told me it had been sold.

He scrubs a hand over his face. "No, we had a rather fast sale, and I handled everything from Vermont with my real estate agent. I didn't see them. They seemed in a rush to move to Florida."

"No kidding," I mumble as I shake my head. When they sold the restaurant, things were tense those last few weeks between my parents and me. They gave me a severance check, for which I was grateful, but I would have preferred the chance to buy the restaurant. It was already a done deal by the time they'd told me about their plans.

I felt them pulling away from Freedom Pie the past few years, allowing me to manage it while they traveled. But I always felt close to them and that they loved me despite their sudden decision to take away everything I loved in one fell swoop. And I can't blame them. The restaurant was theirs, so it was their decision. They seem happy in Florida, and selling the business meant they could live out their dream of retirement there. The restaurant life burned them out, and they didn't want that for me. But I want that for me. Not the burned-out part, but the restaurant life. It's truly my passion. And I can build it myself again.

I couldn't do anything about it, so I moved out to the Golden Gable Inn above the garden shed. My parents said it was emotionally hard for them to sell it, so they just needed to rip the bandage off and let it go quickly. *And that they sure did*, I think grimly.

And then I let my anger fuel me into making decisions that are now altering the course of my life. I place my hand on my belly and feel the baby kick and turn over. I look over and realize Beau is watching me, so I quickly move my hand and straighten my baggy chef coat that's concealing my belly. My pregnancy is none of his concern. *I'm here to do my job*, I remind myself. I don't want him to potentially not want to work with me if he knew. The less personal things he knows about me, the better.

"So you think it'll make a difference?" Beau asks, looking

at the wood-fired oven that takes up most of the kitchen.

I look at him like he's nuts. "It's the *only* way to make good pizza. You need to learn this. Come here." I reach for his arm and pull him closer to show him how I get it going. He watches intently, and he's close to me. He's warm, and he smells good. Mostly like basil and oregano, but it's good. And when I pull him closer, his bicep is huge and hard under my hand. I almost wanted to keep my hand there, but that would have been super weird. If I'm going to work with Beau, I'll need to be incredibly professional.

"This is how you'll make everything from now on. You'll be able to taste the difference, the texture will be amazing, and you'll make pizza that will make everyone come back for more," I say as I get the fire going and wait as it heats.

He peers in and watches the stove and every step I'm taking, and I can see the wheels turning in his head as he's thinking. A look of excitement fills his eyes.

"What are you thinking?" I ask as I watch him in fascination.

"This... thank you. I mean, I felt so lost when it came to all of this." He looks relieved.

"You're welcome," I mumble as I adjust a few things. I prepare the pizza pans and review his supplies, gathering everything we'll need.

It feels surprisingly good to help him, but I'm still salty that he's here and I'm not. I used to dream of him selling this place back to me, and now I'm here helping him. It doesn't make sense, and when Ophelia and I talk about this tonight, she'll probably tell me the same thing and wonder if I need my head examined. He's turning out not to be the jerk I thought he was.

"Alright, show me what you have for supplies." I step away as the wood-fired oven gets hotter.

"I should have plenty of supplies since we've been slow," he says as he shows me the walk-in and storage room. He's right. He's well stocked. And organized. I blink in surprise and dismay. Honestly, I don't think I've ever seen the restaurant this clean, and I'm meticulous. My parents were a little bit more chaotic than I was before they let me run things on my own.

Beau watches me intently, waiting for me to speak. I've noticed he's quiet and doesn't speak much. "What?"

"It's just...very clean," I lament.

He runs a hand nervously down his chef's coat and nods. "I clean when I'm anxious," he admits.

And judging by the look of the place, he's been very anxious. The once darker grout is now light. "Okay," I say as I pull a typed-up plan out of my pocket and hand it to him. "I made a menu and went over it with Beth. We have an official plan."

His shoulders seem to relax as he scans the paper and nods. "We can do this. It's a lot of work, but we can handle this."

"I've been doing this since I could reach the counter. I know we've got this."

He nods, and his bright green eyes meet mine. He stares a little longer and makes me squirm a bit. I wonder what he thinks about when he looks at me. Does he see a practically homeless woman who doesn't have a stable job and makes questionable life choices? Ironically, we're standing in the same spot where my parents told me they had sold the place. When I began to sob, they accused me of making a big deal out of it. They said they wanted me to go out and chase my dreams. They didn't understand that *this* was my dream. I love it here. This was what made me happy. And they took that away from me. They didn't give me a chance to buy the place. I would have figured it out. I wanted this.

"You okay?" he asks as I snap my attention back to him.

"Yeah, let's get started." I tilt my head to him. It's ten o'clock, and I don't want to freak him out, but word is out that I'm back here today, and I think he's about to get slammed with customers. It's a good way to break him in and see what he's capable of in the kitchen.

He runs a hand nervously down his chef's coat and nods. "I'm nervous," he admits.

"We'll start with the basics. I'm hungry. You're going to make us a pizza." I smile at him slyly.

"What's your favorite topping?" he asks.

"Today it's the Freedom Valley Special," I declare as I reach into his giant bowl and pick up his pizza dough that feels off in consistency. "What *is* in this?" I wrinkle up my nose in disgust as I smell it.

"I used a recipe off Pinterest," he admits. "I've been trying out every pizza dough recipe I can find."

"Pinterest?" I look at him and shake my head with disdain. "No. Just no."

He looks at me sheepishly. "Show me the way, boss."

I throw the dough in the trash across the room. "Dough first. This is the only recipe you'll ever need, and you won't find this on Pinterest."

I rummage through his pantry and grab what I need, laying it all out as Beau watches me closely. "Do you want to write this down?"

He grabs a pen and notebook, folding over a page. "Yes, good idea."

I go through the recipe and make five times the amount because he's about to get busy in here, and he'll be glad he has this dough going. He watches me intently and makes notes as I give him instructions.

"Okay, you're going to do the next batch." I slide down and make room for him.

He steps up close behind me, but off to the side, and watches over my shoulder as I knead the dough and roll it out, stretching it. I reach out and put his hand in the dough and show him. "See, this? You want the consistency to feel like this. If it's any other way, it's not right."

His breath tickles the back of my neck as he shadows me, his presence large but comforting. He feels electric standing this close next to me. There's an electric tension in the air as Beau clears his throat and steps back.

I watch Beau work and knead the dough, fascinated by the quick work his big hands make of it. He folds and pounds the dough with strength. The pregnant hormones must be kicking in again because I'm feeling turned on just watching him make dough.

We get the dough done and rising, and he looks pleased and hopeful.

"Ready for sauce?" I ask as I set out all the ingredients.

"Yes," he says as he watches me intently and takes notes. He asks questions every so often and updates his notes. He's adorable with his notepad and pen, but I don't tell him that. I love that he's taking it seriously.

"Normally, we'd let the dough rise longer, but we'll work with what we've got. Today, we'll make more for tomorrow. You always want to prep for the next day. It'll make your life easier. Let's make your first pizza, and then you can make more dough."

"Why would we make more dough?" he asks, confused, looking at all the dough rising.

I laugh. "Because you're going to need a lot more than

that, buddy," I say as I nod to the front of the restaurant. People pour in and look back into the kitchen, hopeful and smiling and waving when they see me standing next to Beau. He just looks surprised and shocked.

"Welcome to Freedom Pie," I call with a smile.

I'm home.

For now.

CHAPTER 9

Beau

The kitchen feels different with her here. Like going back in time to your grandmother's warm kitchen with good smells and comfort foods that leave a memory on your soul. Except instead of my grandma, it's a gorgeous, smart-mouthed, hazel-eyed distraction taking up residence.

A pot of hearty red sauce bubbles on the stovetop, and when I return from emptying all the trash, the aroma in the kitchen almost sends me into a food coma. I'm still dying to know what seasonings she put in there. Just having her here for a few hours has made a huge difference in the place. Every seat was full in the dining room, and for a while, we even had people waiting to eat. To-go orders have been pouring in.

Holly looks so happy, like it's her natural place to be. I watch and try to picture what it was like for her here before I bought the place and proceeded to almost run it into the ground. I'm embarrassed by what I've been feeding everyone. Since she's been here and has been showing me how basic and simple it is, I realize that I overcomplicated the shit out of it all. It's not that complicated. And it sounds cheesy, but the secret is love. She really does pour love into every pot of sauce, batch of dough, and meal she creates. Just watching her, I'm inspired to do better and make this place amazing again.

I was slightly concerned when she was rooting around in her deep Mary Poppins bag and came up with unmarked little jars of spices and seasonings that she set on the counter.

"What are those?" I ask curiously.

"The secret ingredients," she says ominously.

I frown at her. "What are they?"

She chuckles. "I can't tell you *exactly* what they are. That's *my* family secret. They are a mixture of fresh herbs from Mellie's Garden that we preserved just for the sauce. Trust me, you'll taste the difference."

"So you won't tell me the exact ingredients in the seasonings?"

"Absolutely not," she says seriously. "I'll help you get your dough mastered, but I won't share my secret sauce recipe.

But I'll make it for you while I'm here. This is what sets my family's restaurant apart from all the others."

I wait for her to tell me that she's just joking, but clearly, she's not telling me. I'll just have to figure it out myself. It can't be that hard, right?

She's been very patient with me, teaching me her recipes to an extent, something she doesn't have to do, but regardless, she has still been generous with her knowledge and tips. I don't take any of this or her time for granted. I could honestly hug her I'm so grateful. But that would totally be weird and probably freak her out, so I just keep bringing her food and drinks while she works.

I look over, and she's humming and smiling, her hand on her belly over her white chef's coat. When I was in the Army, it was my job to notice people and pick up on their verbal cues and especially their nonverbals. And she has a lot of things that I'm noticing about her.

The other night at the tavern, nobody talked about the fact that she's pregnant, something she's obviously trying to conceal. It isn't my business, and I shouldn't care, but I'm curious. If she wants to conceal it, I'll play along and make sure she gets the breaks she needs and try to anticipate what I can do to make things easier for her without letting on that I know. I wonder what the story is. Hopefully, she'll share it with me. I wonder where the father is and why he doesn't seem to be around. Maybe he'll show up. I had asked

Hank, and he just shook his head when I asked if she had a boyfriend. He didn't elaborate, but I'm guessing he knows more but won't say, making me even more curious.

First, she had me master making the pizza dough while she pounded out pizzas for our lunch rush. I tried to watch and do what she did, but she was so incredibly fast and efficient.

Then she had me mix up several batches of sauce and tasted them before she added a few ingredients and finally declared them perfect. And she wasn't wrong. The spices she brought made a big difference. The next time I see Mellie, I'll thank her and make sure we get more of her spices in bulk if we can. Once I figure out what the exact spices are, that is.

The first pizza we made in the wood-fired oven turned out like no pizza I'd ever tasted in my life, and I'm a self-described foodie. I can see why people love this place and miss the original pizza. If I had her pizza and then was subjected to the nasty pizza I had made, I'd be mad, too.

I start on a pizza, and she leans over and puts her hand over mine. An unfamiliar zing zips through my body when her warm hand touches mine. "Hold on. Let me show you a trick. You put cheese down before you put the sauce down. It makes the crust stay crispy and not get soggy," she says as she demonstrates. She's in her element teaching me this. Her face is flushed, and she looks happy.

I repeat the process she just showed me, and she nods

with approval. Working with her has been surprisingly fun. Honestly, she looks too happy to be here to give me a hard time.

Charlie and Emma, the servers I hired, are happy to have customers and report that we've had a steady stream of happy customers all day long, no matter what the time was. Just word getting around that Holly is back draws people in. We have less than a week now to get everything sorted out and get the food ready for the wedding. I can't let Evan and Beth down. They're taking a chance on me. And most importantly for reasons I still can't make sense of, Holly is taking a chance on me, too.

Holly and I work side by side, and I notice she hardly takes any breaks. I bring her glasses of water and little bowls of veggies and meats I'd cut up for her. She looked surprised at first, but smiled, thanked me, and ate all the food. I encourage her to sit and relax while she instructs me, and surprisingly, she does. She props herself up on the tall stool in the corner by the kitchen bar. She eats her snacks and watches me, offering tips as the day progresses. I take notes, and she shakes her head and chuckles. I don't care. I want to get this right.

"So you really weren't a cook in the Army?" she asks as she pops a piece of pepperoni in her mouth. "You seem to know your way around the kitchen for someone who wasn't a cook."

I look at her and think carefully about my words before I respond. I'm usually not good at talking about myself. But something about the way she asks, I can tell she cares, and it makes me want to open up to her and trust her. She's trusting me by helping me here even though she's gatekeeping the sauce recipe.

"I started out washing dishes at a local diner when I was fifteen to save up for my own car, and by the time I was eighteen, I was running the line cooking," I say as I make another pizza and pick up the big wooden paddle to put it in the wood-fired oven, which has been making the perfect crust. When you bite into it, it has the perfect crisp, chewy crust with buttered garlic. Best pizza I've ever tasted. I can't wait to practice and make even more.

I glance over at her again, and maybe it's the relief pulsing through me that I'm making this work, but I take a chance and open up to Holly since she's taken a chance on me and the pizza shop secrets.

"I love cooking and do it every single chance I get. It's always been a passion of mine to feed people," I say as I add more veggies to her bowl.

"Thanks." She smiles as she reaches for the bowl. "What made you join the Army?"

I clear my throat. "My parents were killed at the end of my senior year in high school, and Hank was only fourteen. It was a month before my graduation, and then it was just

Hank and me. I was already eighteen, so I joined up so I could become Hank's legal guardian and keep him out of foster care. I couldn't let that happen to him."

Her eyes soften, and she looks like she could cry, and she says sadly, "I'm sorry about your parents. What were they like?" She holds up her hand. "I'm sorry. If you don't want to talk about them, you don't have to."

I swallow and move over to clean off the island. "I like talking about them, and I miss them. I think about them every single day. They were great. The kind of parents kids dream of, I guess. My mom was a stay-at-home mom. She loved to cook, and that's probably where I got it from. Hank and I were in every sport you can think of. Hockey, baseball, basketball, football, track, you name it. She rarely missed any of our games. Sometimes we were in two different sports at a time, and it was a full-time job for her to make sure we got to where we needed to be with everything we needed. We always had a ton of energy to burn off, and she kept us busy. It was fun."

"What are their names?" she asks as she leans forward like I'm about to tell her the most fascinating thing.

I smile because my mom probably would have liked Holly. I could picture Holly talking to her in the kitchen when she cooked. She liked to batch cook every Sunday, so we had plenty of food to eat all week. I remember sitting at the kitchen counter sampling everything and keeping her company. "Claire. And Terry was my dad."

"What was your dad like?" she asks as she swings her legs and watches me add toppings to a pizza.

"He was a firefighter like Hank. He was the chief and a good one too. He worked hard and died far too young." I let out a deep breath. It feels surprisingly easy to talk to her.

"They sound great. I'm so sorry they were taken so young. That must have been so hard for both of you," she says.

"It was, but we made it. When I was in basic training and AIT, Hank stayed with one of our old neighbors back in Vermont."

"I'm sorry, what does AIT mean?" she asks, popping an olive in her mouth.

"Advanced Individual Training. It's training for my specific job in the Army."

"Oh, okay."

"Then when I was done with training, he moved with me to my first duty station. He finished high school on the Army base, and he moved back to Vermont to go to school to be a firefighter." I clean off the counter and look out. I see that it's finally slowing down, and we're catching up.

"Why'd you get out?" she asks as she sips her water.

"I wanted a family. But that didn't work out," I say as I scrape the counter and get it ready for the next order.

Her face falls as I say this, and her expression becomes unreadable. I wonder if she wanted the same thing and is missing the father of her baby. Maybe I'm wrong to assume, but I can't figure out why she's alone.

"What happened, if you don't mind me asking?" Her hand instinctively goes to her belly; she still seems to be hiding under her baggy chef's coat.

I check the pizza and roll out the next pizza, feeling anxious to tell her this, the things that make me feel vulnerable and less. "A woman I had met, Nadia, when visiting Hank, and I had a very short-term relationship. She told me she was pregnant when I was back at my duty station from my leave. I got out of the Army and moved back to Vermont to marry her and have a family."

Her eyes widen slightly in surprise, but she doesn't say anything, so I continue. I catch myself revealing things I wouldn't typically share, but something about Holly makes me feel safe with her. Like she can handle the hard stuff. Something tells me she's going through hard stuff now, too, and being with her makes me feel less alone.

"After I got out of the Army, she said she had lost the baby. We opened a restaurant and ran it together until I caught her cheating on me, and we got a divorce. I later found out there never was a baby. She had told me that she was pregnant to manipulate me into moving back to Vermont and marrying her and funding her restaurant. She got the restaurant in the divorce, so I moved here with Hank to start over."

I look over at her, and her face is frozen in a tornado

of emotions. "Holy shit, Beau. I'm sorry. She sucks. Just completely sucks." She shakes her head with disgust and looks angry for me.

"You're gonna need a mop for all that tea," someone says from behind me and look up to see Hank stepping in the back door and stomping the snow off his boots.

Holly hops off her stool and walks over to Hank and gives him a hug. "Hank, how are you?"

Jesus. Why does he get a hug? I want a hug.

"Can't complain. I've been hearing all over town that I need to come by and taste the best pizza in the world. So here I am." He grins.

"You could help out if you want," I say as I swat him with a kitchen towel.

He tilts his head at me. "You *really* want my help in the kitchen?"

"Yes!" Holly says.

At the same time, I say, "No!"

He throws up his hands and laughs. "So how did you get Beau-Beau to spill all his past to you? He's never done that with anyone," he declares as he snags a breadstick from a basket and moans when he chews it. "So good, Hol."

"Never call me that again," I growl. But when I look over, Hank and Holly are engaged in a laugh that makes me feel jealous.

Hank has always gotten along easily with others and is

a people-friendly guy, whereas I'm the opposite. I've been compared to a grumpy, ornery, stubborn introvert, and that's honestly just who I am. I prefer to be in the background, keeping watch and taking care of the people I love. I will admit that I want to be the one to make Holly laugh and smile the way she's comfortable around Hank. Then I realize my brother's face is lit up, and they're talking about Ophelia and how much he likes her.

"Let's talk about you, Holly," I say, changing the subject and inserting myself back into their conversation. "What are your parents like? And you," I say as I point at Hank, "can do the dishes."

Hank salutes as he cheerfully rolls up his sleeves and begins on them.

"Their names are Frank and Maris, as you probably know from the restaurant sale. They had me when they were in their mid-forties. I was their surprise baby as they like to call me," she says as she stands beside me and mixes more dough. She smells good. Like vanilla and coconut.

"What was it like growing up here?" I ask as I roll out more dough and look over at her.

Her mouth turns up as she gazes off like she remembers something. "It was incredible. I have so many memories here."

"Why didn't your parents give you the restaurant or let you buy it?" I ask as she reaches over and grabs some of the dough to roll out.

Her face drops a little. "My parents were convinced I was only here working with them because I felt obligated to stay. They wanted me to get out and try new things and pursue what I wanted. But the truth is, this is all I've ever wanted." She shrugs with a sad smile. "I love it here. I love cooking, being around all the people and families celebrating milestones, and being in a place that makes memories. This place was my passion. When I'm here, I'm happy."

Guilt fills me, and I don't know why. I want her to be happy, and I hate that we took that from her, even if we didn't know.

She continues. "I didn't have enough money to buy them out at the time, and I think they knew that. But they also didn't give me a chance to try to figure it all out either," she says as she swallows and looks down at her plate that's now empty.

I slide out fresh cheese sticks and slice them up and drop three on her plate and nudge it over to her.

"You don't have to keep feeding me, you know," she says with a grin as she takes a bite of one. "Oof, hot. But these are very good. You've got this, Beau." She moans approvingly as she covers her mouth.

Hank dries his hands on a towel and comes over and swats me back with it from earlier. "You can keep feeding me," he says as he swipes a cheese stick and dunks it in some sauce

I've laid out.

I lean back and stare at the now empty restaurant, our first actual lunch rush in the books complete. It feels good.

"I knew putting you two together was going to work out in my favor," Hank teases as he points a cheese stick at us.

Holly rolls her eyes. Her eyes dart to a dark shadow that flashes in the corner, then her eyes come back to mine.

"You saw that, too, right?" I ask her, panicked. I really think I'm starting to see things here.

"See what?" she asks, her eyes on Hank, who is laughing.

They're messing with me, and I can't figure out why, but I will.

The timer dings, and I take out the last pizza for a pickup order.

I look over at her. "What you said about the restaurant and it being your passion? It's my passion, too."

Compassion fills her eyes. And something else I can't decipher. I watch her and can't seem to take my eyes off her. I like having her here. It's been the best day so far. Holly's beautiful and kind, and I want her to keep talking to me.

"What are your dreams for this place?" she asks, looking genuinely curious.

"This is finally something that I want. Not what I have to do for everyone else. I want something nobody can take away from me. I lost my parents, my other restaurant, and who I thought was my family. This is for me. I meant it when

I said this is my family's legacy. I'm creating something here for me and my future family."

This seems to shock her. Her face is unreadable. Then she nods, and I realize she understands. I think we want the same things. Maybe she could be my partner here.

I look over, and Hank is smirking at me.

CHAPTER 10

Holly

"Holly! Beau! I'm here to help. Where are you?" Ophelia calls from the front of the restaurant as the bell on the door dings. We're closed but left the door open for a few takeout orders I'm wrapping up.

"We're back here," I call as she steps into the kitchen, sliding off her gloves and stuffing them into her coat pockets, taking in the organized chaos of hot food containers stacked and ready to take to the wedding reception.

"Wow," I say as I look at her. "You look beautiful, Opi." Her hair is curled in waves around her shoulders, and she's wearing a beautiful soft gray sweater dress with black tights and tall black boots. Her usual makeup-free face is flawlessly made up, and she's stunning. She's a natural beauty, but she looks so confident right now, and I love seeing her like this. "You're a smoke show. Where's your firefighter to put you out?" I tease.

Beau snorts and shakes his head, trying to hide his grin.

"What?" I tease. "You know they adore each other. And they're so cute together, too."

"Holly…" Opi scolds and draws out like we should know this. "Hank and I are *just* friends."

"Sure," I tease. "Hank doesn't look at me like he looks at you, and I'm his *friend*."

Beau tenses and mumbles something about Hank better not be looking at me like that but moves to carry boxes in thermal bags out to the Suburban we borrowed from Logan and Allie for the wedding food transport, making eye contact with me.

Interesting.

I'll dissect that reaction with Opi later.

After the door shuts behind him, Opi looks at me and grins smugly. "He likes you."

He likes you.

I try to wrap my head around what this means. I'm still wrapping my head around becoming an unexpected mother. And figuring out what my identity looks like now. Beau makes me feel things. He's very attractive, sure. I would have to be blind not to notice that. But that's not it. What is attractive about Beau is his heart. The way he's vulnerable and a good brother and a good person. His dreams are attractive. He loves to cook and he loves Freedom Pie. Almost dare I say as much as I do. And that is attractive. And this baby throws a wrench in everything for sure. And now I'm wondering what Beau thinks when he looks at me.

Okay, later is now. "You saw that too, right? That was interesting."

"Interesting, indeed." Her eyebrows rise. "How's it been going?"

"It's been fine. We're just busy getting the catering job done."

"Hmm." She smirks.

"He's unexpectedly cool," I admit. "Want to help me package up these containers of pasta. They must go from the pans to the truck. They're kind of heavy for me," I admit.

"Of course, and you'd better not be lifting any of these, anyway," she says as she starts packing the pasta containers. She pauses and says, "He knows you're pregnant, right?"

I shake my head and look nervously at the door.

"Holly! You have to tell him. This is a physically demanding job, and you can't keep working as hard as you've been." She scolds me, her face scrunching up with worry.

"I will. We've just been busy," I say guiltily.

"Don't you think he suspects? I mean, it's becoming more and more obvious," she says with her eyes widening and head tilting. "Just sayin'."

I shrug. "He hasn't asked."

"I want to talk to you about something. Don't get mad," she pleads.

"What?" I say, bracing for bad news.

"I can't let you dog groom anymore."

I close my eyes. Great, another job lost.

"In fact, I think you need to consider taking it easy, my friend. You can't keep working all these jobs like a crazy person. You need just one job, and you need to take it easy and be normal. I will help you with whatever you need."

I breathe out a deep sigh. "Thank you. I know. Preston and I talked about it. I need to find a place to live and a solid job. The game has changed now, and I have to prepare to be a single mom. I have so much to figure out. It's overwhelming," I say, stretching. My back already aches, and we still have so much work to do tonight. I'll likely be on my feet all night. My to-do list is never-ending now. I need to find a daycare, pack a hospital bag, oh, and learn how to be a mother. Just a few simple tasks, I think with a flash of panic.

"What about working here? Can you see if Beau needs you permanently? I know it's not exactly what you wanted, but at least you love it, and maybe he would even give you maternity leave, or hold your job for you after you have the baby."

"I don't know if he'd want me to work here after this

catering job," I say wistfully. "It's his dream now, not mine."

"You don't know unless you ask him. It seems to be going good for you both so far. You haven't killed each other yet." She shrugs, stacking two of the pans of food. "Think about it."

"You're probably right. I'll think about it," I mutter.

"What did you say?" she teases over her shoulder as she heads out to the SUV. "Say it louder…"

I roll my eyes, and Beau holds the door for her and comes back to grab a few pans. His eyes meet mine, and for a moment, I wonder if he heard us. I hope not. I don't want to appear desperate to him, and I don't want to talk about the baby with anyone yet. I know I'll need to soon because I can't keep hiding it forever, but today is Evan and Beth's special day, so I'm just going to focus on making it perfect for them.

We get everything loaded into the SUV, and Opi says she'll meet us at the barn on the Nolan property next to the inn where Evan and Beth will be having their snowy winter wonderland-themed wedding. Beau helps me into the SUV because the snow is really coming down, and I'm grateful. I try not to wince when I get in, and his eyes are on me full of concern.

The drive to the inn was surprisingly quiet. Beau isn't super chatty, but if I get him talking, he seems to be opening up. I snuck a few glances at Beau, hoping he didn't notice. He's got his dark black chef coat on and dark pants that make his butt look amazing when he bent over loading up the SUV. When he strained to pick up the large thermal food containers, his corded arm muscles looked so good. Too good.

We pull up, and horse-drawn carriages are set up to bring guests from the parking area to the barn. Thick heavy plaid blankets cover their legs as they ride up to the barn decorated in lights and lanterns lined up with garland and snow. This looks straight out of a Hallmark movie, only better. I love Freedom Valley, and I love that Beth and Evan have this for their special day. It's so cozy in the winter barn decked out in snow and greenery and candles.

My breath hitches. "This is so beautiful," I say softly, looking around at the setup.

Beau backs the SUV up to the back of the barn, where we set up the food and warmers for the Italian-themed buffet. It's not traditional wedding food, but nothing with the Harpers is typical. People have their own traditions here, and that's one of the things I love about Freedom Valley. It's unique, special, and these people are like my family. This is why I didn't want to move to Florida with my parents. This is home to me, and I love it here. It's special to me, and there's nowhere else that I'd rather be.

My heart twinges a little when I think about my parents, clueless about my situation. I wouldn't say we're in the best place, but I'm not mad at them. I know they did what they thought was best, and ultimately, it was their business. I know I need to come clean with them about the baby. They deserve to know they're about to become grandparents. I've hid it well because when we FaceTime, they see me from my chest up, so they can't see. But even then, I hide my bump well under baggy hooded sweatshirts and then my chef coat when I'm working. Ophelia is right. It's getting harder and harder to hide it. And soon it will be a living, breathing human so there's definitely no hiding that.

When the wedding starts, we have everything ready, so Beau and I stand in the back and watch. I have goose bumps as Pete, the inn handyman, walks Beth down the aisle, kisses her cheek, and gives her away to Evan, who beams at his bride in his black tux. Beth has a beautiful long-sleeved lace wedding dress on with a long white train. I've never seen a more beautiful bride. Her long blond hair is curled in waves, and her bright red smile lights up the whole place. I love seeing them so happy. Nobody deserves a happy ever after like the Harpers. They are good people and have always been so good to this town. Beth and Evan coming together has been an incredible epic romance story to watch unfold. They are truly made for each other. They even included the inn dogs, Chip and Bossy, in the ceremony. Opi helped get them ready for when they made their way down the aisle, making everyone smile.

Allie and Logan held Benny and Eden, the twins who slept through the ceremony, but everyone still cooed over them when they said their vows with the babies asleep on their aunt and uncle. Benny wore a little black tux, and Eden had on a little light pink dress.

My mind drifts off, and I think about what my baby will look like. Will she love little dresses or little overalls if the baby is a boy? Will he or she love making pizza like I did as a little girl? I think about little onesies I can buy for the baby for the summer and picture cute little chubby baby thighs and perfect chubby rosy baby cheeks to kiss. My heart fills with warmth as I imagine this baby here in my arms, and I get to proudly carry the baby everywhere and do fun things with him or her.

"They look really happy," Beau whispers as we watch, interrupting my thoughts. I picture what Beau would look like holding a baby, making my stomach dip with nervousness and desire.

"Yeah, they do." I swipe a tear from under my eye, trying not to mess up my makeup.

"Are you crying?" he asks wryly, reaching into his pocket and handing me a tissue.

"I'm sorry, weddings make me emotional. Don't you just

love weddings?" I say softly.

"No," he says, his mouth in a firm line.

"Why?" I whisper in shock. "Who doesn't like weddings?"

"They're unrealistic. Most marriages don't even work out," he whispers back.

My jaw drops, and I look at him in shock. "Not true," I whisper.

"For me, it was," he whispers and shrugs.

"Maybe you just haven't met your person yet," I whisper.

A look passes over his face that I can't decipher, and before he can respond, the wedding music cues up, and we have to hurry to prepare for the food and ensure everything is still warm.

We head back and wait for the guests to start gathering. Beau and I are both busy and moving nonstop. As we move, sometimes he'll move behind me, and his hand will settle on my lower back as he comes through. "Behind you," he says softly. His touch is comforting and reassuring, and I didn't realize how much I missed being physically touched with this pregnancy. Just a hug makes me emotional, and I need it.

During the reception, Opi waves at me and comes over, Hank following her like the super cute and sweet Dalmatian that he is, in his firefighter uniform. I look out, and the firetruck is here with the whole crew.

I grin. "How are you guys?"

"We were invited but are on shift, so we just brought the truck. Can't stay long," he adds. "The food looks amazing. You two outdid yourselves."

"Thank you." I smile proudly, looking at Beau, and his mouth turns up slightly in response as he talks to a wedding guest.

"Good, this is beautiful, isn't it?" she says, looking around at the beautiful barn decorated perfectly for a winter wedding. "If I could ever dream up my own wedding, it would be just like this. The only thing I would add is more dogs."

"It really is," I agree. "And yes to all the dogs. By the way, how's the new dog training program coming along?"

"Really good. I'm fully booked out through March now," she says with a big smile.

I nod but try to hide a yawn with my hand. I am dead on my feet but don't want to say anything. I need the money from this job and don't want him to think I can't pull my weight.

Beau turns and says something quietly to Hank, and watching them and their side profiles, both so similar looking, yet their personalities so different.

"We're going to have our happily ever after's someday, too, you know," she says as we both watch Hank and Beau.

"I love that for you," I say, stacking pans and wiping down the table, ignoring the part about it being an us. I'm not sure if that's in the cards for me.

"Who knows, maybe we can marry brothers," she waggles her eyebrows.

My eyes widened in shock at her and cut to Hank and Beau, who thankfully didn't seem to be listening.

"Shhh," I say, turning to her. "Don't say that."

"What? I wouldn't mind being a Sutton. I'm just sayin'. Good-looking brothers right there," she says with a grin, looking at Hank as he laughs at something Beau says. They both look happy and relaxed together.

I roll my eyes but grin, holding back another yawn. Today was exhausting but fun. It's bittersweet having the wedding and catering job come to an end. Two things I was looking forward to. I need to figure out my next move with finding a stable job that I can do for the rest of my pregnancy, and while I'd love to keep working with Beau, I don't want him to give me a job out of pity.

We worked well together, and I had fun. Surprisingly we didn't kill each other. He's not the troll of a man who I thought he was. He's...complicated. Surprisingly sweet and incredibly attentive underneath that surliness. He kept bringing me food, reminding me to drink water and take breaks. He doesn't even know I'm pregnant, yet he took care of me in the way I needed it. He listened and took notes when I taught him something and genuinely seems to love Freedom Pie. I want to hate him, but honestly...I can't. He's wonderful. I close my eyes in exhaustion.

"Hey," Beau says, and I snap my attention to him and waver on my feet.

"Yes?" I say, pretending not to be exhausted.

"Why don't you head home before it gets worse out there. Hank and I have the rest."

I shake my head in protest. "No, I'm okay. I'm committed to finishing the job. It's only fair."

Beau's eyes lock on mine, and he says softly but firmly, "You're dead on your feet. You need to go home, and you know it."

I look away and try to hide a yawn. "No, Beau. I'm alright," I say stubbornly as I turn and start packing up food containers.

Beau looks pissed, and he says something to Hank, who looks over at me and nods. "Get your coat, Chef. I'm taking you to the inn," he demands firmly as he holds my arm and gently pulls me to the door with him. He feels warm and strong, and I have no energy to argue with him. I'm about to melt into him and have him carry me, I'm so exhausted.

Beau whispers in my ear, "Holly, just please don't fight me on this, okay?" And his breath is warm and sexy, and I'm stunned for a minute, and all I can manage is a nod. I like him being this close to me. I realized how much I missed having someone touch me, be near me.

Opi tosses Beau my coat and hands me my purse. "Get her home safe. It's really coming down out there," she says conspiratorially. "I'll help Hank."

"Thanks for all of your help, Opi," I say as I zip up my coat that now strains over my swollen belly. Beau reaches for my hand and guides me out to the SUV that's already warming up before I can make up an excuse to stay.

He helps me into the truck, and I sink into the heated seat, exhaustion overtaking me. Beau reaches across me and places my seat belt over me, our faces close as he buckles me in. Close enough that he could kiss me if he wanted to. And I'll admit, I think about what it would feel like. The thought is a welcome distraction from the soreness and exhaustion my body is screaming at me for. My feet and back are so sore that I can't go on for a single minute longer. I hate that he's right. I need to go home. I can't keep going at this pace. Pregnancy is now officially physically kicking my ass. Things do need to change. I drift off feeling peaceful as soft music plays in the warm truck. I look out the window as snow comes down in big chunky snowflakes. Today was good. A good, exhausting day that filled my cup with all the people I love. I should be happy, but I'm worried. Beau's and my partnership could be coming to an end. He hasn't said anything yet about moving forward working together. I feel like if he knows I'm pregnant, maybe he won't want to work with me. I tried to prove this week that I'm fully capable of being his co-chef. If he decides it won't work, I won't be able to cook at Freedom Pie or have a reason to see him anymore.

CHAPTER 11

Beau

I pull up to the inn, and I'm unsure where to take her. Ophelia said to take her around the back. I was shocked when they said she lived above the garden shed. Who the hell lives in a garden shed in the dead of winter as pregnant as she is? I don't like this. *What the hell?*

I picture her living next to a rake and a dirty shovel, and the thought of that makes me want to just take her home with me. I have an entire apartment just for me now, and it doesn't make sense if she gave all of that up to live in a garden shed.

I figure out where it is and get as close to the door as quietly as I can while she snores softly in the seat next to me. The short drive took a little longer than usual because I had to take the main road because the side roads through the property were too snow packed, even with the four-wheel drive SUV. No way she could have made this drive in her compact car. And the fact that she's made this snowy drive to the restaurant every day and back doesn't make me happy either.

Evan told me it was unlocked, so I head in and turn on the lights before I carry her in. I look up the steep stairs that go to the loft and immediately don't like that she's going up those stairs either. But I'm relieved it's not a typical garden shed but more of an updated barndominium that seems actually very nice. *Okay, no dirty shovels, but still. Those stairs.*

I open her door quietly and reach in and throw her purse over my shoulder, unbuckle her, and pick her up. She murmurs and burrows her face in my neck, mumbling something incoherent.

I carry her up the stairs and lay her on the bed. I pull off her shoes and unzip her coat, sliding it off her as she turns and curls onto her side, her chef jacket slides up, her undershirt showing the outline of what I expected she was hiding underneath it. A small round baby bump.

My heart squeezes tight like a vise. I look around, but there are no personal items anywhere. Just clothes neatly folded on top of a suitcase. She's been living here for months and never really unpacked. It's just a place to land. And not that I have any room to talk at the apartment. It's hardly decorated, but for some reason, this makes me sad for her. I displaced her, and she has no real home now. And where is she putting this baby? They deserve to have a stable and solid home. *And how is this my business?* I ask myself. It sure as shit isn't, but I want it to be, and I don't know why. I've known her for a week. But I want to be near her. This has been one of the best weeks of my life. And I've been disappointed that it's coming to an end. I've been racking my brain all night trying to figure out a way to convince her to keep working with me at the restaurant.

She stretches and looks exhausted, mumbling. "Thanks, Beau. For everything."

"No problem," I say softly.

"Beau… I have to tell you something."

"What's that?"

"I'm pregnant," she whispers softly.

"I know," I say as I lean down, gently brushing a curl of hair from her cheek, tucking it behind her ear.

"How did you know?" she asks, looking confused.

"I just noticed. You don't have to hide anything with me, Holly," I say quietly. She looks so vulnerable lying there, and for some reason, I feel the urge to pull her in my arms and tell her it will all be okay. Even if I don't know that. Something in me wants to make it all okay for her.

"Thanks for doing the catering job with me. I'm going to

miss working with you," she says softly.

I clear my throat and just come out and say it. "What would you say to staying on and being my co-chef?"

"I don't need a pity job. I'm fine on my own," she says. "I didn't tell you so you'd feel sorry for me and offer me a job."

"It's not a pity job, and I don't feel sorry for you. You're a great chef. Cook with me. Let's help each other," I offer. "I need you more than you need me."

She's still for a moment, and I'm nervous about what she'll say. I hope she'll say yes, but seeing how stubborn she is, it could go either way.

She nods with what looks like tired tears in her eyes. "I'd like that."

"See you tomorrow, chef," I say as I shut the door softly and head out.

After I slide back in the SUV, I lean back against the seat and exhale. I finally feel like things in Freedom Valley might just work out. This week was the best week I've had in years. I felt challenged and hopeful.

I need Holly. This isn't a pity job at all. If anything, she's taking pity on me by helping me. Without her, I will sink this ship. She's the one saving me. She's seemed happy the past several days working with me to get everything ready. We were a well-oiled machine this week. We got it done, and we had fun. I need more of that in my life, and so does she.

I drive back to the barn to pack up and wonder where the

father of her baby is and why he's not helping her. And what about her parents? I have so many questions, but now she'll be working with me, so maybe I'll be able to find out.

I back up to the barn, and Hank, Opi, and I load everything up, and they jump in.

"Holly get home okay?" Opi asks, looking over, shivering as she tries to get warm.

"Yeah, she fell asleep on the way. She was so exhausted," I say as I pick up a load of containers.

Nodding, Opi pulls out her phone and scrolls.

"Who all knows she's pregnant?" I ask them, lowering my voice.

Hank looks away, and I immediately know that he knows.

Opi looks at me with narrowed eyes. "What are you talking about?"

"She told me."

"She told you?" Opi asks incredulously.

"Yeah. I'm guessing it's a secret, and she's not telling too many people."

"She's not," Opi says. "Hank only knows because she passed out at the school, and he was the paramedic who responded."

Hank looks at me sheepishly. "I can't talk about work. You know that."

"She passed out? What the hell?" I frown. "Is she okay?"

"She's okay but needs to find a solid job that will work

with her for the rest of her pregnancy," Opi says with a smug grin. "Know anyone who would want to hire her?"

"As of tonight, she's agreed to be my co-chef," I say, still fuming about her passing out and then working as hard as she did all week. I wish she'd taken even more breaks than I'd convinced her to take now. When she comes to work next week, things will change. I'll make sure of that.

"She didn't tell you because she thought you wouldn't hire her. She's been working odd jobs all over town and needs something reliable with better hours."

"I'll make sure she has what she needs," I clip.

And I will because she's not passing out on my watch.

"Look at you being the protector of Holly, your former archenemy." Hank grins, and I glare at him.

"You'd do it, too," I argue. "And we were never enemies."

"You definitely had the whole enemies to...what, friends now thing going on," Hank says as he stacks in containers next to mine.

"I was never her enemy," I reiterate.

"Well, you had a rough start. But I'm glad to see you both worked that out. I like Holly," he says.

I do too. It's hard not to like her.

CHAPTER 12

Beth: Thank you all for helping make our day so unforgettable. Love you guys!

Allie: Officially my sister now. Love you, too!

Mellie: It was so beautiful and so much fun. Love you both!

Paige: The wedding of the decade. So beautiful and the food was so amazing, Holly!

Me: Thank you! I'm so glad the food all worked out.

Allie: We saw you leave with Beau. And neither of you killed each other. Good job!

Me: Haha. He actually asked me to work with him as his co-chef permanently.

Mellie: Say, what?! Yesssssss.

Beth: That makes me so happy! How do you feel about it?

Me: I'm happy. I missed it. :(

Allie: I think it'll be good for you.

Opi: It is good for her. She was the happiest I've seen her in a long time this week being back.

Me: Thanks, guys. When do you get back from your honeymoon?

Beth: Five days. I already miss the babies. We're on our layover in Houston. Hawaii will be a much-needed tropical break from our snowy Freedom Valley.

Mellie: Have so much fun and take pics!

Beth: Will do.

I creak open the back door of Freedom Pie, still feeling like an interloper knocking on my old door, but it is what it is. It's not mine anymore. I hear Zach Bryan playing on a speaker, and it smells good in here. I hang up my coat and bag and look around at the clean and organized space. I take a deep breath, feeling good to be here.

I step into the kitchen, and Beau's got his back to me, sliding in a pizza to the brick fire oven. He's singing softly.

He turns and sees me, and his mouth turns up slightly. "Good morning, Chef."

I'm nervous seeing him after our moment last night. He

carried me to my bed and all but tucked me in. I confessed I was pregnant, and he offered me a job. A part of me wants to make sure I didn't dream any of that up.

"Good morning. I wasn't sure if I dreamed up your job offer or if that was real last night," I admit, looking at all the pizzas laid out across the counter that he's making.

"It was definitely real," he says as he hands me a small bowl of pasta and a fork. "Here, try this."

"What is all this?" I motion at the pizzas lined up all over the counter space.

"Thanks to you," he says as he grunts and picks up a huge stack of pizzas. "We are swamped with orders. Word has gotten out that you're back in the game. People have clearly missed your cooking, and they're making up for lost time."

I take a bite of the pasta and cover my mouth. "Oh my God, what is that? You made that? That's fresh."

He nods. "I love making homemade pasta. The flavor is like no other."

Warmth fills me, seeing him so passionate about the food he's making here. "You should add that to your menu. Immediately."

He looks over. "You think so?"

I nod as I finish the last bite and wish there was more. "Yes. Absolutely, yes."

"Well, we'd better get to cooking, Chef." He smiles at me and turns back to the wood-fired oven.

I admire the view as he strains to lift a big pizza out of the oven. "What do you need help with?"

He slices the pizza he's working on and slides a piece onto a plate and hands it to me. "I want you to try this and give me honest feedback," he asks proudly.

"Alright," I say, picking it up and taking a bite. Covering my mouth, I lean back and moan a little. "Beau, you did it. So good. You don't even need me here anymore."

He scoffs and shakes his head at my comment as he wipes his hands on a towel and smiles proudly. "Of course I still need you. Look at what you've done to help me get this place alive again."

He's still for a moment, watching me. Then he slowly reaches over and wipes the corner of my mouth with the pad of his thumb. His eyes slowly draw from mine, and he looks away almost as if embarrassed by his action. My mouth is warm where he touched me. I try to keep from blushing, secretly loving his touch.

"It's very good. Just the way Freedom Pie is supposed to taste. Great job," I say, clearing my throat, nervously taking another bite and nodding. "You don't have to keep feeding me, but this is tasty. Thank you." I smile.

"Thank you for your help," he murmurs as he cuts himself a slice. The corners of his mouth turn up, and I can't help but notice the tingles I feel while watching his mouth.

"Of course. Teamwork makes the dream work," I reply.

Lame. Jeez, why am I so nervous around him all of a sudden and saying dumb things?

He wipes his mouth. "The school ordered twenty-five pizzas today for an event. Want to help me drop them off?" he asks.

"Absolutely. That's great for your business," I say, almost saying "our" instead of your because it still feels so strange that this whole place is his, and I have no ties to it now other than being a co-chef. He could let me go at any time, and I'd have no say in anything. It's so different from being the one running the place.

"I have a question," he says as he leans up against the counter eating, his long legs stretched out in front of him.

"Yes?" I ask as I try to busy myself making the last few pizzas that he's already gotten started.

"Why aren't there other things on the menu? I found the original menu tucked behind the cash register, and it's still the same back in the eighties as it is today. You guys didn't want to add anything or mix it up?" he asks curiously.

I laugh a little. "I always wanted to add things. I went to culinary school and came back with so many ideas, but my dad never wanted to update the menu. He said he liked things simple, and my mom agreed with him. As you can probably tell," I say as I glance around the entryway to the dining room at the dated decor. "They weren't big on change."

He nods thoughtfully as he looks around. "What would

you add to the menu if you could mix it up?"

I take a deep breath and smile broadly. "I have entire menus saved on my computer that I've played around with and dreamed up over the years. I have Pinterest boards of how I would have changed the decor in here." I look around, remembering the plans I'd dreamed up. "I had big dreams for this place."

"I'd love to see them," he says earnestly.

I turn to him. "Yeah?"

"Yeah," he agrees. "I would love to update things and add more things to the menu. I think the town loves what we offer, but it would be fun to experiment and add in more options."

I can't even hide my smile. "I can help you with that," I offer.

"Let's make it happen, then," he says excitedly. "We can talk about it later when it dies down after lunch."

I chuckle. "If it's anything like it's been lately, it probably won't die down, but I can show you what I was thinking later."

"Deal," he says as he grins at me, and my heart swells in my chest.

I may not have my restaurant back, but I'm here, and this makes me happy. I'll take it.

We get to the school, and they have carts waiting for us to take the pizza in to the cafeteria to set up. When SJ sees us, he waves and comes out to help us. "Let me get the door, guys," he says as he helps.

"Hi, SJ, how are you doing?" I say as I follow him down the hall.

"Great, now that you're here. These kids are excited about the pizza party. The overall consensus is the kids miss you here, Holly, but they're glad you're making pizza again."

I laugh. "I'm glad I'm making pizza again, too."

SJ helps me load the pizzas onto the cart and smiles.

"What are you doing over here at the elementary school?" I ask as I roll the pizzas on the cart.

"Just filling in for the PE teacher. She's on maternity leave," he adds.

"Ah, that's nice of you," I say as we wheel everything into the cafeteria.

I've known SJ all my life. SJ and his dad, Sam, have been weekly customers for as long as I can remember. Sam is the town mechanic, and SJ works for him part-time and coaches full-time now at the high school.

Beau brings in the rest of the pizza, and we get everything set up. I look over, and he's crouched down, talking to a few of the kids and making them laugh. I overhear him, and he's lit up and animated. "Are you guys excited for pizza?"

"No," a small boy says with an angry frown.

"Why not? It's cheese pizza," Beau offers with a friendly smile.

"Cheese makes me angry," the kid says with a loud growl and picks up one of the lunch trays and throws it across the room. Luckily, no one was hurt, and the teacher takes the little boy off to the side.

Beau snorts and looks at me with surprise. "That was…"

"That's a first," I admit. "Life *without* cheese makes me angry."

Beau looks back at the kid, who gives Beau the finger, then back at me. "That kid is going places. Maybe not Harvard… but places."

I laugh and start to set the pizza up for the kids. I look around and try to picture my baby attending here someday, and I can't see it. It's so strange.

Another kid walks up and asks, "Do you have cauliflower pizza crust? My mom always makes my pizza with cauliflower crust."

Another kid chimes in, "Cauliflower smells like toots."

I snort laugh, and Beau tries to hold in his laughter as well.

It's cute seeing him interact with little kids. When I first met him, he seemed so grumpy, and now, I'm rethinking everything I thought about him. Looking back, he was losing his dream and struggling. I'd be grumpy too. *I was grumpy.* This partnership with Beau is exactly what we both needed.

"Hi, Miss Springs, I'm so glad you aren't dead," Toby says with a toothless grin.

"Thanks, Toby, me too." I smile, not quite sure how to respond to that statement. But at least the kid isn't freaked out that I passed out as his substitute teacher.

Another kid gets their plate of pizza and says, "Do you make pizza now because you got fired for almost dying?"

I clear my throat. "I didn't almost die, just passed out. That happens to people sometimes, and now, I am making pizza, not teaching," I say, holding back relief that I'm not here anymore. It wasn't my favorite.

"My mom says she's glad you're back because she says the new guy's pizza sucks," another kid pipes in.

I look over at Beau, and he grits his teeth and smiles.

Another little girl says, "Well, my mom wants to know if you want to be my new stepdad?"

I can't even hold back. I laugh so hard, I'm shaking. SJ's eyes are wide, and he looks like he's wheezing from trying not to laugh.

"I'm going to walk away now," Beau says as he shakes his head, ignoring the little girl.

The little girl continues. "She's also the school nurse if you want to go talk to her."

"Absolutely not," Beau clips as the little girl shrugs and takes her plate of pizza.

SJ and I exchange another look and chuckle. "You have

some fans," he tells Beau.

My hand goes to my abdomen, and I freeze. A powerful little foot presses against my abdomen, pushing my shirt out with force, causing my hand to hold it.

"What's wrong?" Beau stills as he looks at me.

I shake my head and try to straighten. "Nothing. The baby must be doing a back flip in there right now." Usually, I try not to feel the kicks and put it out of my head and pretend it's not real. I didn't want to form any emotional attachment to the baby because he or she wasn't supposed to be mine. Only now, I am the mom. And warmth fills me as I picture an actual baby that will soon be mine. I won't have him or her taken from my arms. Little pepper will be staying, and I will be this baby's mom. A massive, happy grin is on my face, a sense of pure contentment washing over me.

Beau surprises me when his hand twitches like he almost puts it out to feel but instead flexes his arm, straightens it, and stands. "As long as you're okay," he says, his eyes on me.

I'm almost tempted to take his hand and let him feel it because it is cool, but that might be weird, so I just nod. "Yeah, I'm fine."

"Alright, ready to get back for the lunch rush?"

"Let's go," I say as I turn and wave to SJ, who waves back and heads out to the truck. I'm already tired, but I'm not telling him that. It feels so good to be back.

CHAPTER 13

Beau

Evan: Hey guys, I added Beau to the text thread.

Evan: Thanks again for the help with the last-minute catering. It was all so great, and we appreciate you and Holly.

Me: Our pleasure. Thanks for the opportunity.

Evan: How did it go working with Holly?

Me: Surprisingly well. I'm finally getting customers back in. She's going to be working full time here now, and my pizza doesn't suck, so there's that.

Evan: Glad to hear it. You're doing a great job. I think you'll work well together.

Me: Thanks for the nudge. It's definitely going better than expected.

Logan: Aren't you supposed to be on your honeymoon? What are you doing bothering us? Lol

Ty: Yeah, where's your wife? Shouldn't you be doing honeymoon things?

SJ: Dare I ask...honeymoon things? (Shudders)

Preston: I think there's a law against not enjoying your honeymoon and texting your freezing friends back at home.

Evan: Oh, my honeymoon is fully being enjoyed. My wife and I are currently lying on the beach with drinks and watching the waves roll in.

Selfie of Beth and Evan holding drinks doing cheers in bathing suits in the sun.

Me: Okay, that's just making me jealous. It's snowing here again, and you're on a tropical beach. WTH lol

Logan: When you come back, let's plan a guys' night and catch up. You better come too, Beau! You're in the circle now.

Preston: Just say when. I'm down.

Hank: I'm always down!

Me: Hank, how did you get in this group before me?

Hank: I have an in with Ophelia.

Logan: Get along, pizza brothers.

Hank: Can we please find someone for Beau so he stops being so grumpy?

Ty: Mellie took this picture.

A pic of Beau and Holly in their chef jackets on the wall at the wedding, looking at each other and smiling

Hank: That'll do. ;)

I save the picture to my phone and smile.

I head downstairs to meet the delivery driver and realize he was early and had already left the boxes on the porch with a sandwich baggie of nuts and dried fruit on top. A note is under the bag:

For Stephen.

Okay, weird. Who or what the hell is Stephen? I make a mental note to ask Holly and show her the baggie. If they're feeding a rat, I swear to God, I will lose it. I'm already convinced we have rats. I've never seen a rat or any evidence of rat poop, but something is going on. At first, I thought maybe I was just tired and seeing things. But now I'm determined to figure out what it is.

I scan the alley, looking for Holly's car, and wonder what time she's coming in. It's later than usual for her, and I check my phone for a text.

Holly: Roads are snow packed, so I'll be a little later than usual. Waiting for a ride.

Me: Where are you? I will come get you.

Holly: Thanks, but I have it taken care of.

Who the hell is giving her a ride? Hell no. I turn to go inside to grab my keys to go find her, and Hank swings his truck in and pulls to a stop behind the building and honks obnoxiously at me as he usually does. Holly sits in his passenger seat and gives me a small wave. She turns and laughs at something Hank says.

Relieved that she's here safe, I realize how much I look forward to Holly coming to work every day. We may have started out rough, but partnering with her as a co-chef is one of the best things I've ever done.

A few weeks ago, I wasn't sure if I would make it here, and now I have new friends, business is picking up, and I finally have the Hail Mary I needed to make Freedom Pie finally work. It feels like I can finally breathe. Dare I say I'm happy. I even found myself whistling today as I worked. And that's never happened before.

The truck door flies open, and Hank says, "I brought you a special delivery!"

I open Holly's door, and she gives me the smile I crave. I feel it in my bones when she looks at me like that, and I don't like it when she gives Hank those smiles. I want them all for me.

"It's freezing," she says as she hurries inside and takes off her coat. I hang it up for her and stand with my hands awkwardly in my pockets, not knowing what to say.

"What?" she asks. "Why are you being weird?"

"He's always weird," Hank offers from the kitchen island, where he's likely scavenging for food.

"Just worried when I saw your text. Where's your car?" I ask.

"Stuck in a ditch on the road by the inn. Sam and SJ are towing it back to the inn for me. I picked her up," Hank says as he grabs a drink from the cooler.

"You went in the ditch?" I practically yell, worry filling me. I lower my voice. "Are you okay?"

"Relax, Dad, I had her," Hank says dryly as he assembles a sandwich.

"I'm okay," she says. "Thanks again, Hank. But do you think you could give me a ride home tonight?" Holly's eyes shift to me nervously, as if it was hard for her to ask me.

"Yes," I immediately answer. "I can give you a ride anytime." I give Hank a look.

"Why did you call *him*?" I ask, handing Hank a knife to cut his sandwich in half. I'm trying not to be butt hurt that she seems friendlier with my brother than with me. I mean, I get it. Everyone loves Hank. But come on. I want to be the one she calls when she needs someone.

"I was driving by and saw her spin out. I was at Ophelia's," he says with a grin.

"Of course, you were," I say as Holly buttons up her chef jacket, and I notice the buttons are straining and stretching.

"Speaking of…I need a favor," Hank says after he swallows a bite of his sandwich.

"What?" I ask as I make Holly and me sandwiches.

"Can you help me surprise Ophelia with a date night this Wednesday?" He looks at both of us nervously.

"It's her birthday," Holly adds as she grabs a sparkling water for herself and holds one up to me, and I nod.

"I know. I want to make a special dinner for her, but I'm on shift," he adds.

"Then how will you have a special dinner for her if you're working?" I ask.

"Well, I'm so glad you asked, big brother. The dinner isn't for two. It's going to be for six. I'm bringing the whole crew. But I just need a special table set up for me and Ophelia."

"How is that a special dinner if you're eating with your entire shift? This won't be very special," I ask with dismay.

Hank shrugs. "We're just doing it, man. It is what it is. The crew is all on board."

"What if you get a call?" Holly asks. "You'll just leave Opi here? That's not very romantic. Why not just wait until you're off to celebrate?"

"I have it all figured out. Don't worry," he assures her.

I exchange a look with Holly, shake my head, and we both

grin. "Okay, you got it. A special dinner for six."

"Anything you can do to make it extra special for her, I would appreciate it," Hank says as he chugs the last of his drink. "I'll bring the flowers."

I hand one of the sandwiches to Holly. "It's Hank and Ophelia's world, and we're just living in it."

She looks at Hank and smiles. "He's all in. He doesn't even hide it. I'm so happy for her. Every woman deserves to be loved out loud, fiercely, and proudly. The bar should always be set high."

I don't miss the look on her face. She wants that. She's so relaxed around Hank, and with me, she's reserved. And I know we work together, and she's probably being professional. But I want the smiles and jokes she gives Hank. I want that with me.

Soft music plays throughout the restaurant, and the lights are dimmed, transforming from a family pizza place to a more upscale restaurant look. Candles are lit in small lanterns on tables.

"Think the firefighters will mind the candles or take offense?" she jokes as she stands back and looks at the candlelit room. A table of six is set up in the middle, and a table for two is set up off to the side for Ophelia and Hank. A white tablecloth is laid over their separate table, and earlier, Hank dropped off roses to place them in a vase on their table.

"I think it looks great," I say as I look around at the dining room. A few patrons stop in the doorway, looking confused at the transformed restaurant.

"Come on in, we're open," Holly calls. She guides them to the booth on the side of the restaurant and hands out menus.

I lean in the doorway and watch, not even holding back my smile as I watch her chatting and laughing. I love seeing her smile, and the sound of her laughter, the way her eyes light up with the customers. She's comfortable here and clearly in her element. I close my eyes for a moment when I realize I'm fighting a losing battle with this woman because she intrigues me and captivates me like no other woman ever has. I thought I had this with my ex, and that was never it. Holly is special.

The Freedom Valley Fire Department pulls up and parks out front, and Holly watches with me as they all pile out, shrugging on coats and carrying their radios as they walk in. Holly guides them all to their seats.

"Welcome," she calls as she gets them all set up. Our servers immediately take their drink orders and bring out baskets of warm breadsticks. One thing I've learned is that when people come to my restaurant, I want them to immediately have a drink in their hand and something to snack on while they order. Hank waits in the doorway, watching for Ophelia. I look at him, and pride fills my chest. Hank has turned into a good man, and I see a lot of our dad when I look at him. My dad was always like that with our mom, bringing her flowers and having special dates set up for her, even if it was just at home. We didn't always have a lot of extra money or time with all of our busy schedules, but he made time for my mom. I remember one time my dad doing the same thing, taking my mom on a date with his crew for their fifteenth anniversary, and while I doubt Hank remembers that, it's a good memory to see him doing the same thing my dad had done for my mom.

The door opens, and Ophelia comes in, shutting the door behind her. She looks around and spots Hank and melts, giving him a hug and a kiss. "What's all this?"

"Happy birthday, Ophelia. I wanted to have a special dinner with you," Hank says proudly as he hooks a thumb over his shoulder. "Don't mind those guys."

Ophelia grins as she waves at the crew, who all turn and wave back at her. She turns to Hank and seems to melt. "You brought your whole crew to have a date with me?"

"I hope that's okay," he says, looking shy, not the norm for Hank, which is funny as hell.

I look over, and Holly has happy tears in her eyes as she smiles, watching Hank and Ophelia. I lean down and murmur in her ear, "I'm going to hug you now because I think you need one, but if you don't want me to touch you, tell me now."

Holly steps closer and buries her face in my chest as I wrap her up in a warm hug, pulling her into me, careful of her baby bump. The feel of her head pressed between my collar and jaw is a balm to me, something that has my pulse jackhammering. It's my first time holding her, but I know it won't be the last.

"Sorry, I don't know why this is making me cry," she says softly.

"I like seeing him happy," I say as I don't dare move. She remains connected to me, and I love it.

"We'd better get these pizzas started," she says as she lets go and walks to the kitchen, with me trailing her like a puppy. Hank and I are goners for these Freedom Valley women. And I seemed to fall for the most complicated one of them all. Only it doesn't seem that complicated to me. Holly is amazing, and I want to be around her. I want to help lighten her load and make her smile and laugh. I want to hear more stories of her happy childhood here and learn more about what she wants in life. I'm drawn to her, her beauty, everything that she is, and I've never met a woman quite like her.

Dinner was fun. We made Hank and Ophelia a heart-shaped pizza, salads, and breadsticks, and luckily, there were no fire callouts, so they could take their time eating.

Laughter, music, and happiness filled the restaurant tonight. This is what I wanted. And seeing my brother happy makes me happy.

At the end of the night, after we cleaned up and Holly looked like she was going to fall asleep, I pretended we were done so I could get her home. I'll come back to clean up after she's safely at home in bed, resting where she needs to be.

We head out, and I help her into the truck and slide in next to her. I start the truck and rub my hands together. "It's freezing," I murmur.

"I just need my warm bed," she says as we make our way to the inn. The drive takes longer than normal in the snow, and even in four-wheel drive, my truck struggles.

"Can I ask you a question?" I ask as we turn into the inn and find her now snow-covered car in front of the garden shed, just like Sam and SJ promised it would be.

"Sure," she says as she zips her coat all the way up. The weather is frigid cold, and walking from the truck to the shed is like walking into a deep freezer.

"Do you like staying here?"

She looks at me and tilts her head. "It's alright. Why?"

"Well, I was wondering if you'd like to stay with me at the apartment? Then you wouldn't have to worry about going back and forth in this weather?"

I'm not even sure where this is coming from, but it spills out of me before I can stop it. I want to help her and care for her, and I want to keep her and her baby safe. I have all this room. And to be honest, I'm lonely as fuck up there all by myself. And thinking about her driving back and forth in this drives me crazy.

Holly looks surprised at my question, and she looks speechless. "I'm sorry to bother you with the ride..." she says.

"No, it's no problem. I just worry about you," I admit. "I have all that room..."

She bites her lip. "Thanks, Beau. I appreciate it. But I'm okay." She leans over and gives me a hug. "Thank you for the ride." She looks surprised by my question, but also tempted. Disappointment fills me when she says no, but I understand. I had to offer it. I just want her to be safe.

"I'll pick you up tomorrow. Ten o'clock," I declare.

"I'll be fine," she calls as she stands to get out of the truck, and I hurry to help her to the shed door and hold it open for her.

I follow her up the steep garden shed steps, prepared to help her if she fell, which she doesn't of course, but I can't help but worry about her on these steep steps.

She gets to the top of her steps and turns to me in the doorway. "I'm good, Beau."

We face each other, and there's not a lot of room at the top of the stair landing, so we're close, and our eyes meet. I swipe my thumb across the apple of her cheek, where she has a smudge of flour.

I reach down and take her gloved hand and hold it in mine. Lifting it to my mouth, I press my lips softly to the small expanse of skin on her wrist that peeks out between her glove and the sleeve of her coat.

Her eyes dilate and soften, and her mouth turns up as she watches me, her lips slightly parting at my touch. She says nothing, just stares in a look of desire and happiness.

"Alright. Ten o'clock," I say quickly, turning and jogging down the steps before she can argue.

CHAPTER 14

Holly

I was very wrong about Beau. He's not a jerk, and he's not that grumpy. Okay, a little grumpy. He's like a cat. He'll let you know when he wants to be near you, talk to you, and touch you. And that hug? How is it possible that hugs can make such a difference? I was feeling so alone, and that hug. I needed that hug deep down in my soul. It's crazy how a simple hug can make me feel so much better. I lean my forehead on my cold steering wheel as I sit outside the law office, waiting for my meeting with Preston.

I'm fighting the way I feel for Beau. Every day I am around him, I like him more and more. Beau is so handsome, it's unfair. He is tall, broad, and hard, but he's got such a good heart underneath his gruff exterior. I love that he can be in a grumpy mood, and I can pull him out with a laugh and goofiness. I love when he tips his head back laughing, and I sometimes wonder how the skin on his neck would taste if I kissed him there. I like him in so many ways. And it's becoming increasingly harder for me to be around him and not want him.

My life is such a shit show that I shouldn't be thinking about having any sort of relationship right now. I need to focus on my baby and finding stability. If things were to go south with Beau, and I lose this job, I'm completely screwed. I can't imagine figuring out childcare for a newborn while working all the odd jobs I have been doing.

And when he suggested I stay with him in my old apartment? I wanted to pack my stuff right then and there and go. I want to go home, but it is not my home anymore, and I'd be a guest. If things didn't work out, then where would I go? I need to keep a boundary with Beau. It's hard because I already feel like Hank is a brother to me. But Beau? The way I feel about Beau is not in a brotherly way. Oh no. I wonder daily what it would be like to kiss him and have him hold me. The other day, I dreamed that Beau was holding me, and when I woke up, it was just Bossy, the black and white inn dog, I borrowed for the night spooning me. But damn that was a good dream.

I look over and see Paige coming across the street holding

a drink carrier of coffees and a bright blue bag from Baked Inn Love bakery. She waves at me and holds up the bag. "Hi, Holly! I got us coffee and cinnamon rolls," she says as she sets the bag down and unlocks the glass door.

"Good morning, let me help you," I say as I take the carrier from her, and she smiles gratefully.

"Thanks, let me just get situated, and I'll let Preston know you're here. He's been here working while I did paperwork over at the bookstore. We really need to hire a new receptionist but haven't been able to find someone. I'm helping him out until I can get someone in here full time for him." Paige owns the bookstore, and Preston has his own law office.

"Thanks. What can I do to help?" I ask.

"Here, a decaf latte." She hands me a coffee and pushes the bakery bag across the desk to me. "Make yourself comfortable, and it'll just be a moment," she says as she heads to the back with Preston's coffee and a pastry from the bag.

How she knows my coffee order, I don't know. I'm guessing Allie told her. There's no better coffee than Baked Inn Love coffee. It's my go-to place.

I hear her voice talking to him and sip my drink and sigh. It's so good. I snag a cinnamon roll and take a bite, holding it to my napkin, and my eyes roll back in my head from delight. I love Allie's cinnamon rolls. When I tell you that there is nothing I wouldn't do for one of Allie's cinnamon rolls at Baked Inn Love, I mean there are literally zero crimes off the table. They're that good.

I look around, and it's cozy in here. It's not what you'd think when you go to a law office, but it's a small-town law office. Preston has been good to the people here, and he's been a huge help. I look at Paige's desk and wonder if she knows my situation. I know Preston has attorney-client privilege with me, and he would never tell anyone about my business.

Paige strolls back into the front office and sits in her chair across from me and sighs. "Alright, let's catch up. How's it going with the pizza brothers?"

I used to squirm when they called them that, but now it doesn't bother me as much because I have got to know Beau and Hank and really like them both now. Feels more like our place than their place. It's weird how the dynamic has changed.

"It's actually going really good," I admit, sipping my coffee. "Thank you for this, by the way."

"Anytime," she says, opening her laptop.

"Do you...know?" I ask her, tilting my head a little.

She looks over at me and gives me a reassuring smile. "I do because I type up his notes. But here, I'm just Paige, the receptionist. When we walk out those doors, I'm Paige, your friend, okay?" She makes a zipping motion with her lips.

"Okay," I say.

"Can I ask you something? As both receptionist and friend?"

I nod.

"Why is this a secret? You know we all would love to help you, right? With anything that you need. And...I can't be the only one who has suspected, even before I knew."

My eyes fill and threaten to spill over with her kindness. "It's just hard. I wanted to do it quietly and quickly and be done and buy back the restaurant or start over. I didn't think this through," I admit.

She nods and listens as I continue.

"I guess I kept it a secret, and I'm not sure how to tell everyone now. I feel...like I betrayed you all or something." I wipe the corners of my eyes.

"You didn't betray anyone. We love you." She leans forward and lays her hand on my arm.

I nod. "I want to tell everyone. I just don't know how. I'm tired of the secrets," I admit, tears pouring down my cheeks like the dam broke loose.

Preston comes down the hall and halts when he sees me crying. Paige looks at him and says, "Come in, honey. We're just talking about the baby and how to tell everyone."

Preston nods and sits beside me, his kind brown eyes watching me with patience and kindness. I'm not sure how I got Preston and Paige as my friends, but everyone deserves a Preston in their lives. He's like a protective grizzly bear for his clients and friends. How he looks at Paige is how I dream of someone looking at me someday. Like she's the only one in the room who matters. Beau immediately comes to mind, and I try to shake that thought off.

Paige hands me a few tissues, and they give me a minute.

"Things have changed now, and I need to make a plan. I need help. Legal help and friend help. I've made a mess of my life." I sniff.

Preston turns in his chair and says. "I'm proud of you. You're one of the strongest and most resilient people I've ever met. Out here, we'll make a friend plan. Then, when you feel like the plan is good for you, we'll go back to my office and make a legal plan. How does that sound?"

I nod, grateful. "Thank you."

Paige smiles. "You're having a baby, my friend. This is a good thing. You won't be alone. I can promise you that. We love babies, and we want you to feel supported."

Preston says thoughtfully, "What's your biggest concern?"

"That I won't be a good mom."

They both shake their heads. "Impossible," Preston says softly.

"What if we have a big party and just tell everyone? We can do it at the bookstore," Paige offers.

"Okay," I say. I have to rip this Band-Aid off sooner or later.

"I hate to be the one to tell you this, friend, but it's starting to become a little more obvious. You can only get away with baggy clothes and drinking water every time we all go out for so long. Everyone probably guesses something is up but isn't saying anything," Paige points out as she sips her iced coffee.

Preston looks at his watch. "Alright, come on, let's go make a legal plan." He looks over at Paige. "Can you please get Pancake and Theo out of my office?"

She laughs and heads down the hall and coos as she picks up her raccoon. She calls for Theo, who is snuggled up in his dog bed in the corner, and takes them back down the hall. "He likes to pretend he's a professional and not a small-town lawyer with a raccoon and dog in his office."

I shake my head and grin at Preston. "I still can't believe you guys have a pet raccoon."

"He's a good boy, but we need to have our meeting and make a plan. They need a bathroom break," he says as he sits at his desk and clicks his pen and flips to a new page on his legal pad.

"Yes, thank you for your help," I say as I sit across from him.

"I reached out to the agency and had a meeting with them over the phone. They are closing down. Did you know that?"

I shake my head. "No, I had no idea."

"Yes, they won't be operating after next month. Without a

fight, they have offered to honor your full surrogacy payout for your medical care and services up until the birth if you choose to keep the baby. I negotiated it slightly higher due to the circumstances, and they countered with this amount," he says as he reaches into a folder and slides over a paper with the small amount on it. I close my eyes. It's money that could change my life, and I could open my own restaurant. But now? The restaurant is far from my mind as this baby coming has consumed my entire life now.

"It's contingent on the agreement that you keep the rights to your baby, and their rights are terminated. There's just one more thing."

"What?" I ask, looking up from the paper.

"They are required to report this to the state, and a social worker has taken your case on to make sure that you are qualified and can financially and physically support the baby."

My heart drops. "What does that mean?"

He continues. "It means we need to make sure you have a stable residence, employment, and a solid support system to show that you can take care of the baby."

"Could they really take the baby from me if they don't approve of my situation?" I ask, concern and fear filling me. "And what do you mean by support system? Will it hurt me that I'm not married or have a partner?"

"It's just procedure with the state and the agency. I think

it's a way for them to cover their bases," he answers. "The surrogacy agency was a small local one. Unfortunately, it wasn't run very efficiently."

"I can't risk this baby going into foster care. I have a job and a place to live. Do you think the garden shed apartment is okay?" I ask.

He nods and makes a note. "I don't see why not. How're your finances?"

"I have a decent chunk in my savings since I worked so much," I admit. "The surrogacy check will help, but I'll have to figure out a new plan to make it last."

It's crazy to think I would have given up every dollar to my name to get the pizza shop back. Now I'd give up every dollar to keep the baby.

"Beau should provide medical insurance after the birth for both of you."

I nod, numb. "I'll talk to Beau about that."

"Not just your attorney, but as your friend, you must take care of yourself, Holly. A support system is going to be critical when it comes to the social worker poking around. They will want to see that you have all your bases squared away," he says as he tilts his head.

I nod.

"Okay, so expect a visit from them at some point. If you want me there when you meet, just text me," he says, and I smile. He agreed to help me pro bono, and I'm so thankful for him and Paige. All of them, really. I need to come clean and tell them what's going on. As friends, I would want them to tell me if they were in my situation. I would like to help.

Just then the door blasts open, and Theo the huge Berndoodle comes in chasing Pancake the raccoon.

Preston closes his eyes and looks at the ceiling. Then he says, "Never a dull moment here." He laughs.

I reach down and pet Pancake, who is attempting to jump into my lap for cuddles, and Theo, who is wrestling with him. "They are so cute."

Preston shakes his head as he watches me cradle Pancake like a baby. "I don't know how you could ever doubt your ability to be a good mother, Holly. You are exactly who your baby needs."

I smile and snuggle Pancake to my neck. "I hope so."

"Hope is not a strategy. You *are* the best mother for your baby."

I stand outside, feeling the snow coming down on my face. It's beautiful outside right now, and Freedom Valley on Main Street looks like a town straight out of a Hallmark movie. It might look different now, I resolve. But it's you and me, kid. I've always wanted to be a mom, but this wasn't how I thought it would go. I pictured a wedding, a father for my children. But I'm finally feeling like I'm able to imagine the baby as real and mine. The details of how we got here no longer matter.

I walk across the street and head into Freedom Pie. The bell on the door jingles as I enter and look around. Beau's not open yet, but the dining room is spotless and ready.

I walk through the swinging doors and find Beau as he leans back against the counter, a mug of coffee held to his lips as he looks over at me and says in an odd voice, "Hey, Chef."

I smile at him. "Hey." Then I freeze. My eyes shoot as wide as they can go. "Uh-oh."

"What's wrong?" His brow crinkles, and he tilts his head. "Anything you want to tell me?"

Stephen is on the center island surrounded by nuts, dried fruit, and various other objects he's collected from the kitchen. He looks like he's playing defense for the Chiefs.

"How did…?"

"Oh, don't worry. We're only breaking about a dozen health code violations here," Beau says, his mouth forming a line.

"I see you met Stephen." I laugh nervously. "Why is he on the counter?"

"So this *is* Stephen," he confirms. "He practically fought me for a baggie of nuts and fruit a delivery guy left for him. And if I try to remove him from my kitchen, he gets *very* angry."

I giggle nervously.

"Why do we have a squirrel in here? And are there more in here?" He looks at me in dismay.

"No, just the one," I say with a smile. "He, uh, he lives here."

"No, he does not live here." Beau clips.

"Why didn't you just put him outside?" I ask, confused.

"I am *not* touching that squirrel," Beau practically growls.

I gulp back laughter. "Stephen, you're supposed to be outside."

"Yes, he is," Beau says as he crosses his arms.

I walk over and scoop him up, and he climbs up on my shoulder. I scoop up his bounty and drop it into a towel and carry him out. I gently place him on the roof and drop his towel full of bounty next to his house.

"I'm sorry, buddy. You know the rules. Dad never let you on the counter like that. You have to be a good squirrel, or you'll get in trouble with grumpy Beau."

"I'm not grumpy!" he calls.

I giggle. "Not at all," I whisper as I stroke his head and body one last time. "Be good."

I head in and wash my hands. Beau sanitizes the island, giving me a playful side-eye.

"Sorry I'm a little late today. It smells good in here," I say as I hang my coat on the hook.

"You're fine. I've prepped everything already, and I made you something," he says cryptically.

"What did you make?" I ask curiously.

"Lunch," he says, looking at his watch. "A little early, but you need to keep your energy and strength up."

He waves his hand proudly to a table in the corner set with dishes and a silver dome covering the plates.

"I had to prepare some of it in the storage room because your little friend commandeered my kitchen this morning."

"So fancy." I chuckle as I look over at the setup and smile with relief. "You didn't have to do all this, but you're right. I'm hungry."

"I just wanted to say thank you for all that you're doing to help me here. I really appreciate it." His gaze seems to touch me everywhere—my eyes, nose, lips—before he focuses on my eyes again. His gaze darkens, his jaw clenching, his teeth sinking into his lip like he's keeping himself from saying more. How does he look at me like this and make me feel like the only person in the room?

I struggle to slide into the booth, and he slides in across from me. Our knees touch under the small table, and he looks at me and smiles. "Sorry."

I'm not. I like it when he touches me. Like, really like it.

He proudly lifts the dome on my plate, and he's made me chicken Parmesan over homemade pasta that smells so delicious and is so beautiful. This man can cook.

"Beau." I breathe in the smells making my mouth water.

"Bon appetit, Chef," he says as he pours water into my glass.

I don't know what I did to deserve this man in my life, but I'll take it.

"Thank you," I say as we eat, and I sneak a few looks at him. His dark eyelashes fan over his bright green eyes as he watches me take my first bite.

"Oh my God, so good," I murmur, covering my mouth with my hand.

I look over at Beau, and he's in rapture, staring darkly at me like he wants to forgo the pasta and eat me instead.

But he quickly changes the subject. "How was your meeting?" he asks.

"It was okay. I met with Preston, deciding on some things about the baby," I admit.

"I need to make sure I have a stable place to live and employment. Which thank you for the job," I say as I twirl homemade pasta with my fork.

He chuckles. "I think I should be thanking you. You helped me turn this place around, Holly. Without you, we were going to fold. I can't thank you enough for saving our ass."

"We're helping each other."

"You know...I still have that apartment upstairs," he says as he looks up at the ceiling and back to me with his mouth turning up.

"So you said," I say, wiping my mouth. "And while I appreciate it, I can't live here with you."

"And why not?" he asks as he sips his water.

"I'm already complicated enough. I can't complicate things even further," I admit. "And besides, Preston just told me that a social worker will be poking around, and I need to be able to prove that I have a stable life for my baby. And if they find out I just suddenly moved in with a guy I just met, that probably wouldn't look good."

"I don't find you to be complicated, Holly. But driving here and back in the snow daily is proving to be complicated, wouldn't you say?"

I shrug. "It wasn't too bad today."

He just continues to stare at me with his smoldering, sexy stare that takes my breath away. Beau freaking Sutton.

He's not making it easy not to fall for him.

CHAPTER 15

Beau

"Can I ask you something?"

"Sure." Holly looks up at me, her eyes meeting mine.

"Where is the baby's father?" I ask quietly.

She freezes, and she says, "There's no father." But I notice she isn't elaborating as she says this.

A feeling in my stomach churns, and I realize it's anger. And a sprinkle of betrayal when I think about what Nadia did to me. Who could leave Holly like this? I *wanted* to be a father so badly, and that was taken from me. Or the realization that it was all a lie. And Holly's here doing this on her own, living above a garden shed.

"What happened?" I try to sound casual as I ask.

She bites her lip, and she looks at me like she's thinking about what to say.

I tilt my head and wait, her eyes softening.

"I was a surrogate, and the parents recently passed away. I had a choice to put the baby in the system or keep the baby. I'm keeping the baby," she adds while she watches for my reaction.

Holy shit. That's not what I expected her to say.

"So there really is no father?" I ask, trying not to let it show that I'm relieved there's no other guy in her life.

"I mean, technically, there was a donor at the agency, but he's anonymous, so no, there's no father in this baby's life. Just me."

And me.

"So this social worker can just come in and decide whether you are fit to be a mother or not? How is that fair?" I question, now worried about her situation.

"I guess. I should be okay."

"I had your health insurance and benefits set up this week, too."

"Oh, good. Thank you for that," she says, looking relieved. "I'll need that afterward, but I'm good through the delivery."

"What if I was the baby's father?" I offer, my hands clenching and unclenching beneath the table.

She swallows her water wrong and chokes, water droplets spraying over the tablecloth. "What?

I shrug, feigning a casualness I don't feel and choosing my words carefully so I don't reveal too much. "I could...be your partner—for appearances. If that's what you need."

Holly wears her heart on her sleeve. I watch her expressions running the gamut, from bewildered, to contemplative, to bemusement. "You want to *pretend* to be my partner and my baby's dad?"

I want to correct her and tell her that there would be no pretense involved for me. I want to be hers and for her to be mine. I want to. But I don't. Not when she needs my help, and I'm able to give it. I just need to keep those pesky thoughts and feelings to myself. This isn't about me.

"If that's what you need."

"A fake relationship for the sake of my unborn surrogacy baby, with the man who I once thought of as my enemy. Not exactly where I saw this day going," she mumbles, her head staring at her plate of pasta like it holds the answers to every problem she's ever had. There's a sinking feeling in my gut like I'm messing this all up. I just want to help her, protect her, and support her. Instead, I'm adding to her stresses.

I reach across the table, my fingers lightly stroking the back of Holly's soft hand. She lifts her head, those startling hazel eyes looking right at me, squeezing my heart in the process. "Let me help you. Please."

"You really want to?"

"I don't make a habit of offering to do things I don't want

to do."

She swallows. "How would we do this?"

"Let me be your partner with whatever you need," I say, leaning forward and meeting her eyes.

"Why would you want to help me like that? My life is a complicated shit show, Beau."

"You don't get it. You have helped me more than you'll ever know with my dream here at the restaurant. You became my partner when you didn't have to. I will be yours because I want to. You have no idea what you've done for Hank and me by helping us out here."

Hank and I were going to lose this restaurant. She came in and saved our asses. I will do whatever it takes to save hers. Be her baby daddy? You got it. Share my home? Move in. Whatever you need.

"I don't know what to say." Her lip quivers. "But why would you want that?" Her voice drips with uncertainty.

"I think we might want the same thing here." I motion to the kitchen and her belly.

She sniffs and looks out over the dining room. "My parents told me when they sold this place that I had no dreams, but I did. Freedom Pie is my dream. They didn't believe me or seem to see me."

"I see you, Holly. And you saw me. That's what partners do for each other."

"So what would this look like between us?"

"You and me? We're a pair from now on. We run this restaurant together, we live together, and we bring your baby into the world together. Partners in it all. That social worker who comes around? She'll have to go through me if she wants to get in the way of you keeping our baby. Because we're going to be partners."

"Partners?" she echoes.

"Whatever you need," I say, my eyes locked on hers so she knows I mean this.

She gulps. "That's...quite the offer."

"You had my back, and I have yours. What do you say?"

She exhales and leans back, her hands resting on her belly, and takes a moment to think about it. "Okay, let's do it," she finally answers hesitantly.

I nod and smile at her. "Okay."

As we stand to get ready for lunch, she turns to me. "Do you want to shake on this or something?"

"Or something," I echo. "I have a better idea." I tuck a wispy hair behind her ear. She leans into my hand for a moment, and I can feel she likes my touch.

I ask her, "Can I give you a hug?"

Her eyes close, and she nods, remaining still.

I pull her into me and tuck her under my chin, putting my arms around her and holding her tight. I don't say anything because to be honest, I'm not sure what the hell I could say after this conversation. She's in her most vulnerable place, and she needs someone.

I hold her for a long time, and she finally pulls back and swipes a tear quickly as if she doesn't want me to see. I turn her to face me. "Hey. What's wrong?"

"I think I just really needed that," she says hoarsely. "Thank you."

"Anytime."

"And...Beau?"

"Yeah?" I say, eyes locked on hers.

"You give good hugs."

This probably isn't a good idea on so many levels. But why did it feel so right to offer all of that? While it's unconventional, we need each other.

I carry boxes in off the delivery truck and set them in the corner by the stock room. She's singing along to a song as she makes a big pot of sauce. Her hair is pulled up on top of her head, and her chef coat is unbuttoned and hangs open. Her belly has stretched it out, and I think she just gave up on buttoning it at this point. We're becoming a well-oiled machine at the restaurant, and having her here has made a night and day difference.

She's focused and has a small smile on her glowing face as she grabs a fresh spoon, dips it into the sauce, and tries her creation. She closes her eyes, breathes in, and smiles.

I cross my arms and lean against the doorframe, watching her. I can't help it when she's lit up with happiness. This is what they talk about when they mention pregnant people glowing.

She turns around and catches me, her cheeks turning pink. "Beau, try this," she says as she grabs a new spoon and blows on it lightly before raising it to my mouth, waiting for my reaction.

I try it and nod. "That's really good. You look happy."

"I am happy." She smiles as she turns back to the stove, still swaying to the music.

I needed her. And it feels good to have her need me.

Holly

He made me a fancy dinner and then offered to partner with me. I'm still not sure what he means by all the partner stuff, but to be honest, I could barely focus because he was like a walking dream.

I will always look at Beau and wonder how any woman before me didn't see what I see. He's amazing. He's loyal, hardworking, incredibly good-looking, and funny. When I'm with him, it feels...right. And good. Even if he's pretending.

He is grateful for me, and he wants me here. When I'm here, he makes me feel like I'm more than a single pregnant mom who needs help. He gave me a job in my favorite place on earth. Sure, it's unconventional, but like I said, I'm complicated, and that doesn't seem to scare him either.

I had been so nervous about my appointment with Preston that I hadn't eaten much besides my beloved cinnamon roll and was so hungry. I ate so much that instead of working, I just want to curl up and nap. But we're working through the lunch rush together, and all of a sudden, he's in my space, everywhere. He steadies me with his arm, hands me things, and our hands brush. His eyes meet mine, and I swear they sparkle.

He looks happy.

"This was amazing. You're a phenomenal cook, Beau. Homemade pasta is the best." I groan, holding my stomach.

"Are you okay?" he asks, looking concerned.

"I'm stuffed. This was incredible. We have to add your homemade pasta to the menu. You're going to ruin store-bought pasta for everyone. No one will ever be able to eat that stuff once they've had this."

"I'd love to add it to the menu," he says as he leans back, watching me, our arms touching again, making me tingle.

I nod. "We can make this happen. I'm excited about the new things on your menu."

"*Our* menu." He interrupts gently.

"Okay," I agree with a smile as I lean back, rubbing my belly. The baby probably isn't happy with the lack of room in there after that meal. "That was the best meal I've ever had," I tell him.

He scoffs. "This is just a random Tuesday. Wait until you see what I make you tomorrow."

My eyes widen, and I laugh. "What's so important about tomorrow?"

"Every day is important," he counters. "And I love to feed the people I care about."

"Well, I'll take it." He cares about me. *Don't read into it,* I tell myself. Just a slip of the tongue. Then I stare at his mouth and picture his tongue and him kissing me.

"How's the baby doing?" he asks, his eyes dropping to my hand on my abdomen.

"Good! Kicking up a storm. Want to feel?" I ask, then suddenly feel shy about asking.

His eyes light up, and he doesn't hesitate to lay his hand next to mine. I move mine on top of his and move it over to where the baby is kicking.

His eyes widen, and he murmurs softly. "Wow. You really can feel that."

I nod. "Sometimes pepper wakes me up at night."

"Pepper?" he asks.

"Short for pepperoni. I just didn't want to call the baby an it," I admit sheepishly.

"So you don't know the gender?" he asks, his eyes meeting mine. My gaze drifts to his mouth and back to his eyes quickly. His mouth quirks, and he continues holding my belly.

"No, I want it to be a surprise."

The back door opens, and Hank and Opi come in. Beau doesn't move; he just looks up at them. Hank and Ophelia break into a wide grin and look at each other and back at us.

"Are you having like a date?" Hank asks with a grin, walking up and scanning the table for food. He settles on the last breadstick, snatches it, and takes a bite.

"What are you doing here?" Beau scoffs at him, but I notice he's set back a meal for him like he usually does. "We're having lunch. And I was feeling the baby kick."

"I want to feel," Hank protests, but I can tell he's joking, as Opi joins him at his side. He's just saying that to get a rise out of Beau as he usually does.

"No," Beau says sharply with disdain. "Absolutely not."

Hank shrugs his shoulders, and Opi and I laugh. Someone is territorial. *Interesting.*

"When can we tell everyone and plan a baby shower?" Opi asks, sliding her hand in Hanks.

"Well, I talked to Paige and Preston, and we're going to have a little get-together at the bookstore and tell everyone."

"Why not have it here?" Beau asks, looking at me curiously.

"I didn't want to volunteer your restaurant," I say softly.

"We'll do it here," Hank says. "We can make pizza and have a little party."

"You mean I'll make pizza," Beau says dryly. "I'm not

letting you anywhere near the pizza again. You almost burned the place down last time."

I laugh when I look at Hank and Beau. They are typical brothers badgering each other, but I can tell they really love each other.

Hank holds up his hands and laughs. "Whoa, whoa, whoa. Stop telling people that." He pretends to be offended. "I'm a firefighter. I put out fires, not start them."

Beau looks at him dryly and says, "You left the wooden paddle in the wood-fired oven."

Opi laughs. "Yeah, let's leave the pizza making up to the experts."

Beau's eyes cut to mine. "Holly and I are going to be officially together now."

Hank's and Ophelia's jaws are dropped and looking at each other. "What? What does that mean?" Ophelia asks, looking at me.

"It means we'll help each other with whatever we need. The restaurant, etc," I add nervously.

"It means that when she goes into labor, I'll be her partner, she's here, and we are together."

"Like...together, together?" Hank asks.

Beau nods. "Holly gets my complete support, just like she's supported us."

"Not the same." I shrug. "But I am thankful for your help."

"You have made this place turn around," Hank says. "And

Beau is far less grumpy, so thanks for that."

Ophelia pulls me to the side of the kitchen. "Are you sure you know what you're doing?"

"Opi, I have no freaking clue what I'm doing, but I'm running out of time. This baby is coming, and if he's offering to help me, who am I to say no," I say.

Hank and Beau laugh at something as Hank helps him break down boxes in the storage room.

"He's like super hot for that," she swoons. "I like Beau, but be careful. I don't want to see you get hurt."

"He's been really great," I remind her. "And if you really are good with it, it would be fun to have an after-hours party here and tell everyone. Although I'm not sure how much of a secret it really is anymore. Paige, Preston, Callie, and you know. That doesn't leave too many people to tell. But I hate not being honest with my friends."

"I think everything will work out. I'll be here whenever you need me. Also, remember what I said about brothers," she whispers and laughs.

"Yeah, yeah," I whisper back with a grin.

We make plans, and Hank and Opi agree to help us with the party. I'm nervous, but it feels good not to feel so alone with this secret. It's crazy that I did this in the first place to get the pizza shop back. Now I'm back, and I couldn't have imagined my life turning out more different. Surprisingly, it gives me hope, and I really like it.

Ophelia: Mark your calendars. This Thursday, we are having a dinner party at Freedom Pie at 8pm. Come hungry and be ready for a big announcement!

Beth: We'll be back! I can't wait to see everyone!

Allie: What's going on?

Ophelia: Can't tell you. Just come!

Paige: Pres and I will be there.

Callie: SJ and I will be a few minutes late. I'm off at 8, but I'll be there shortly after.

Mellie: ohhhh, an announcement! Ty and I will be there.

"What are your favorite toppings this week?" Beau asks, his arms paused over the toppings bar on the prep table.

"Hmm, pepperoni and olives," I say as I sweep the floor in the dining room.

He looks at me as his mouth opens and closes, and he returns to making the pizza, not saying what he thinks.

"What's wrong with pepperoni and olives?" I say as I fight back a yawn. My feet hurt, everything hurts, but I won't tell him that.

"Last week, you hated olives. You said they were an

abomination straight from Satan's loins. That was your exact quote," he reminds me.

"Yeah, well, this week, I love them. I can't help it. The heart wants what it wants." I shrug.

He just looks at me sideways. "You better eat this and not tell me it's gross after I make it."

"Of course, I'll eat it. I eat everything you make me."

"Your baby has you changing your cravings constantly," he mutters.

I put the broom up, straightened my coat, and peer down at his pizza. "What about stuffed crust?"

With a nod, he grabs extra dough and starts rolling it. "Wait, what are you doing?" I ask.

"Making stuffed crust on the top."

"Let me show you," I say as I slide in next to him and show him how I turn the crust to make it stuffed with cheese around the edges. "Here, you try," I say.

He reaches around me and takes the cheese and dough and follows my movements. Our hands brush, and he moves closer to me, standing so close our sides are touching. We're shoulder to shoulder, and my hands move over his, helping him shape the dough so the cheese will work.

Our hands move together in an almost erotic rhythm, our bodies touching, the heat between us a tangible thing. We're so close, so close I smell his intoxicating scent, and it sends my hormones haywire. So close that if I turned my head, I could kiss the five o'clock shadow peppering his strong jawline. As I turn my head, the temptation too strong, Beau glances down at me, his heated gaze trailing a blaze over my face, burning a pathway to my mouth. I lick my lips involuntarily as though I could taste Beau there already, wanting him to kiss me. Needing him to. Just when I'm strung as tight as an elastic band, the tension in the air suffocating us both until our breaths are the only music in the room, Beau leans down until his mouth brushes softly against mine.

He doesn't move. He stays there, just holding me, his mouth on mine. Then he pulls away slightly, and his eyes lock on mine.

"You like my pizza?" he murmurs, still so close.

"I love your pizza," I murmur back against his lips.

"Was that okay? I just felt..." He looks at me nervously, watching my face, something he does a lot. It's like he's reading me like a book.

"Yeah, that was okay. Really okay," I say shyly.

"Really okay?" He laughs and asks, "Can I do it again?"

"Yes, please." I can't hide my nervous grin, but I really want him to kiss me. When he touches me, it sends sparks through my body. When his lips touch mine, it sends explosions through my body.

Turning, he pulls me to him and looks at me. He tilts his head down to me and kisses me softly again. I melt into him, whimpering slightly as he slides his tongue gently across my lip. My mouth opens, and he swirls his tongue against mine. He tastes minty and spicy and amazing. My hands wrap around his waist, pulling him closer to me as he kisses me slowly. His arms wrap around me, pulling me in close.

"Wow," I say as we pull apart.

"Wow," he repeats, leaning against the counter.

"What are we doing?" I ask, taking a deep breath.

"Kissing." He watches my face. "I like you, Holly," he says as he tips my chin up with his hand and traces my cheek with his thumb.

"I'm complicated," I say softly.

"So you've said. Complicated doesn't scare me." He reaches down and spans my stomach with his big hands that cover my swollen belly.

My breath hitches. Beau's body feels like a magnet to mine. I want him touching me, kissing me, and... I want him. Complicated or not. I want this with him.

CHAPTER 17

Holly

"Thank you all for coming," Opi announces as she stands, getting everyone's attention. We all just got our food and sat down. She kept looking at me and knew how nervous I was, and I begged her to just do it and tell everyone for me to get it over with.

"We have a new member joining our crew this winter," she says as she smiles.

"You're pregnant?" Mellie asks, shocked, looking at Hank and her.

Hank sprays the soda he was just drinking, and Beau leans over and claps him on the back. "Way to go, Hank," Beau teases in his brotherly tone.

"No." He shakes his head vehemently. "I didn't get anyone pregnant."

Opi smiles. "I'm not pregnant. But Holly is."

The room becomes quiet, and all eyes shift to me and Beau. Beau realizes they are all looking at him and back at me.

Ty looks at my now more than obvious belly bump that I'm no longer trying to conceal and back at Beau. "Yeah, that math isn't mathin,' buddy."

Beau chuckles and puts an arm around me protectively. "It's not mine either. It's all of ours."

Smiles, chatter, and congratulations break out. I see some confused looks, but they are genuinely happy for me, and I can't believe I thought their reactions would be any different. I'm questioning why I didn't just let them all in on it sooner.

Beth looks over and shakes her head with a wide-eyed Cheshire cat grin. "Thank God we're all finally talking about the pregnancy that we're all not talking about."

"You knew?" I ask.

Beth grins and shakes her head. "Yeah, for like forever. Just waiting on you to tell us what's going on."

"It's not what you probably think. I signed up with a surrogacy company, and things were going well until a few weeks ago when I found out that the parents, whose baby I was carrying, passed away. It was not what I ever could have imagined happening when I originally signed up. The agency is closing, and they said I could keep the baby or put the baby in foster care."

"We would take the baby before that happened," Beth says, looking upset. Beth grew up in foster care when her own mother passed away from cancer when she was little.

"I know." I hold up my hand. "I would never let that happen. I'm keeping the baby."

"So you used a donor?" Allie asks curiously, taking a bite of pizza.

"Yeah, I don't know much about the donor. The surrogacy family got to pick the donor, and all I know is they refer to him as J27. Since the family had trouble conceiving, I donated my egg, so biologically, it is my child and J27's."

"That must have been hard," Mellie says.

"I wanted to help them, so I really didn't think much about it until they passed away, and now, I can't imagine letting this baby go out into the world not knowing exactly where this baby would be."

"When are you due again?" Paige asks, and Allie's and Beth's eyes snap to her.

"You knew?" they ask at the same time.

"Only through work with Pres, and I can't disclose anything from there," Paige says sheepishly.

"I'm due in five weeks," I say. Her eyes widen, and she freezes.

"Five weeks?" she asks. "I can't believe you've been pregnant all this time."

"Yeah," I said softly.

"Well, that explains the decaf you always order." She chuckles.

"Yeah. I'm sorry. I didn't know how to tell you."

Beau turns and looks at me, and it's like he can tell I'm nervous. His hand slides under the table and finds mine. He squeezes my hand and bumps me gently with his thigh.

My shoulders relax despite my skin tingling where he touched me. That kiss has changed things for us. I wouldn't call us a couple, but we're closer. He's more than my friend now. This is getting very interesting.

Dinner was uneventful after that, other than hugs, belly pats, and plans to throw a baby shower that I protested. But these people love me, and I love them. I know they're just excited for the baby and me. And I want them to feel included. Several weeks ago, I was passing out at the news that I was about to become a single mom. And now? Now, I'm starting to feel excited and not as freaked out and scared. It feels good to be loved by the people I love.

After the party, Beau refused to let me help clean up, so I ended up sitting on a pallet of huge sacks of flour in the corner of the kitchen. Beau hadn't had time to put it away before the party. I sat there talking to him and Hank while they put the dining room back together. Everyone pitched in and cleaned up before departing for the night. I listen to Hank and Beau banter like brothers and talk about Hank's house and other stuff. Before I know it, I find myself drifting off to Beau's voice and presence wrapping around me, keeping me warm and safe. It's not that I'm exhausted here. It's that the pizza brothers have given me a haven, friendship, and comfort. I'm relaxed enough to drift off because I'm in good hands. I need to just rest for a moment.

CHAPTER 18

Beau

"I'm going to take off," Hank says. "I have an early shift at the station."

"Thanks for all your help."

"You sure you know what you're getting yourself into?" He looks at Holly in the corner. She's fallen asleep, leaning back on top of the pallet of flour holding her stomach, looking peaceful.

"Yep," I mutter as I take off my apron and adjust my hat backward on my head.

"She's a nice girl," Hank agrees. "You're good together."

I look over at Holly, and my heart melts. She wanted to help so badly, but I convinced her to rest briefly. I had a feeling she'd be out like a light before long.

Hank takes off, and I lock up behind him. I pick up Holly, who is completely zonked, carry her up to my apartment, and deposit her onto my bed. The baby kicks gently as I carry her, and my heart warms. And while others might wonder if I know what I'm getting myself into, I know exactly what I'm getting myself into. If I get Holly, I get two of them. I've been down this road before, and it left me broken and a mess. This time, I can't explain it, but it feels good. It feels right. And I may get my heart broken again, but I can probably take it. Holly and this baby have become important to me.

I slide off her shoes and tuck her into my bed.

Why I feel so drawn to her, I don't know. I'll protect them and be there for them as long as she'll let me. Which I hope is for forever.

She doesn't wake up. She just curls into a ball on her side and snuggles into my pillow, breathing softly.

I close the door softly and take the couch. There was no way she was making it all the way back to the inn tonight as exhausted as she was.

I lie there thinking about what the next five weeks hold. What will it be like when she has her baby? Will she stay here in Freedom Valley? What if she decides to leave and move closer to her parents? She hasn't mentioned that, but we have a lot to work out.

This is new, but I really like her and want to see where this could go. Baby or not, that doesn't bother me. I've always known I was meant to be a father. Whether that baby is biologically mine, I will still love them. I think I already do. Just as I'm starting to slip ever closer to completely toppling over the edge with my feelings for Holly, I need her. She's one of the funniest, kindest, and incredible women I've ever met. She's made my head spin with feelings for the past several weeks. I've felt things I've never felt for anyone before, even with my ex. I thought I loved Nadia. But this feeling with Holly is different. And I am here for all of it.

She wants me. She'll have me. She needs something. I'll give it to her. I'll give her the world if she needs it.

She lights me up. Hell, she powers the fucking sun for me. I'll never admit it, but I even like her damn squirrel. I'm just not touching it.

Holly

The sun streams in my window, and I stretch and run my hand over my belly. "Good morning, baby pepper," I whisper and yawn.

Then I sit up and realize I'm at my old apartment. *Beau.* Where is he? I smell coffee and food cooking.

Relief and happiness fill me when I remember where I am. My old home. It feels good to be back here, and I'm with Beau. My heart swells, and I want to run and hug him.

I duck into the bathroom and see he's left out a new toothbrush for me. My heart warms. Of course he did. Beau thinks of everything.

I wash my face and brush my teeth, and when I come out,

Beau is cooking in a white T-shirt, gray sweatpants, and his hair is messy. He looks like a walking snack.

"Hi," I say softly, leaning in the doorway.

"How did you sleep?" He looks up at me, and his eyes soften as he flips a pancake in a pan.

"Good." I smile. "Confused me at first when I woke up. I haven't slept good like that for months. It felt like I was home for a minute. Thank you for letting me stay."

His expression is unreadable, but I can see in his eyes that he's thinking as he listens to me.

"I hope you're hungry. I made blueberry pancakes, bacon, and scrambled eggs."

"It smells good. Thanks," I say as I reach out of habit for the plates and find the cups. I close my eyes. It's so strange to be here with his stuff here now. A reminder of what I lost but a reminder of a new friendship.

Opening a cupboard, he hands me two plates and brushes his lips against my forehead. He says nothing, just squeezes my arm gently as he scoots by me. Somehow, he seems to feel my emotions and understand.

I'm suddenly nervous here with him in his space. Nothing happened between us, but sleeping and waking up in his space and having him take care of me feels so intimate.

He sets a plate down at the small table. "Here. Eat, Momma," he says softly.

Momma. I smile at that and sit.

"You really are a fantastic cook, Beau," I say as I look at my plate and back to him. "Am I 'Momma' now and not 'Chef'?"

He fills his plate and sits beside me, our knees touching again. Something so simple as our knees touching makes me swoon. I love Beau touching me, period. "You can be both."

Both. I have been thinking a lot about my identity lately and who I'll be now that everything has changed.

His love language is definitely physical touch. He's always holding my hand, touching my shoulder, and I admit that I love it. I freaking love it. I didn't realize how much I missed basic physical touch. I mean, I hug Opi sometimes, not much because she's not as touchy-feely of a person as I am. But I totally am, and I can tell Beau is too.

He takes a bite and chews and looks at me, and then says nonchalantly without missing a beat, "I think you should move in here. Today."

I cover my mouth, startled. "I'm sorry, what?"

He shrugs. "It makes sense. You're here most of the time, anyway, and I don't like those stairs at the garden shed." He says this so casually, like he just suggested I make cheese sticks instead of breadsticks.

"I can't just move in here," I exclaim, shocked. "Beau."

"The weather's been bad," he says, his deep voice softening. "I want you here, Holly. We're together. Partners," he reminds me.

"Staying here one night or even two with the weather?

Fine, that makes sense. But moving in here permanently does not make sense. Do you even know what you're saying?"

Nodding, he takes another bite, looking at me and waiting for my response. He's calm and steady like he's already thought this out.

"I'm having a *baby*. A baby that's probably going to cry a lot. I'm like a whole family over here," I say, waving my hand at my baby bump and back at him. "You're like a whole bachelor over there. These are two vastly different lifestyles."

He takes another bite, looking as if he's probably not going to take no for an answer no matter what I say. "I thought we talked about this. We're partners."

"Yeah, but I didn't think you were serious about me moving in here," I admit.

"Beth and Evan said they'll bring your things if you want." He reaches behind him to the counter and grabs the orange juice and pours us each a cup.

My jaw drops. He's serious.

He holds my gaze. "This will be good for you. You can take naps on your breaks. And I have the extra room."

I look around and think about bringing my baby home here someday. Nostalgia fills me, thinking of my baby in the same place I was brought home from the hospital as well.

"Why would you want to do this?" I ask him.

"Holly, I've already told you that you've helped me so

much. I want to help you."

He sets a glass of juice in front of me, his eyes soft on mine, waiting for an answer.

"What if it's too much for you? Then where will I go?"

He shakes his head. "You'll never be too much for me. When that baby cries and you're exhausted, who do you think will hold the baby and help? Me, I will. And you will have help from all of us, Hol," he says firmly.

Picturing Beau holding a newborn does things to me. He's illegally attractive, and if I live here with him, what am I going to do with all these feelings for him? I'm nervous because I'm very pregnant, and I don't feel very sexy at all.

"Wouldn't you like to bring your baby home to your old home?" he asks thoughtfully as he looks around.

"More than you know," I admit softly.

The words lingered in the space between us.

He reaches over and pulls my chin to him and kisses me softly. "Okay," he murmurs.

"You're a really good guy, Beau."

"Don't tell anyone," he teases. "I have a reputation to uphold."

"Which room would be mine?" I ask as I look down the hall and see a faint fading of where pictures of me as a kid used to hang on the wall.

"Mine," he says as I look at him, his eyes burning into mine. "My bed is the best, and I like having you near me.

You can pick either of the other rooms for the nursery. If you want the baby to sleep in the same room with us, that's fine, too."

I gulp. "Oh," I squeak.

His hand covers mine. "I like holding you."

I like holding him, too. He makes me feel safe, secure, and wanted. I've only had a few serious boyfriends, and none of them ever made me feel the way Beau does. They were boys. Beau is a man. He treats me the way I watched my father always treat my mother.

Guilt fills me when I think of my parents and how I need to come clean with them. That's the biggest elephant in the room I've been dreading.

"What?" he asks as he scoots my plate to me, reminding me to eat.

"Just thinking about how I'm going to tell my parents about the baby," I admit. "And you."

"They don't know?"

I shake my head.

"I'm sure it'll take a minute to adjust, but they'll be happy for you."

"One of the reasons my dad wouldn't even consider selling me Freedom Pie was because he said I needed to go out and live my life and not be strapped down to the restaurant for life. When I tell them this, it will seem like I'm a nutjob," I say, defeated.

"Why would they say that?" he asks.

I shake my head. "Beau, I wanted my own restaurant so badly that I became a surrogate. Then when that fell through, I got a job back here, moved in with the new owner, and lived like they never sold it. It's freaking weird. What will they even say to that?"

He doesn't even try to hide his smile. "The baby's coming in the next few weeks. They sound like they love you very much and they will love their grandchild. They're not going to care when they see the baby and see that you are happy," he says firmly. "And if they do, they can deal with me."

He's probably right. My parents are good people, and they do love me. Regret fills me, and I wish I'd told them what I was doing, but they probably wouldn't have liked it. Hearing him be protective over me and my baby makes me fall for him even more.

"Can I kiss you?" he asks, looking at me like he's been waiting his whole life to do it.

I swallow nervously and nod. "You sure?"

"I want to do a lot of things with you, Holly, but a kiss is definitely what I want right now."

"Why would you want all of this?"

"I want you to be mine. And your baby."

And then his mouth lands on mine, and this time, it's not gentle. It's needy, and he kisses me like he means it. Suddenly, I am no longer as confused about Beau. He wants me, and I want him. The math might not be mathin' to some people, but it feels right when I'm with him.

Beau

I'm deep in thought working when I see Holly step into the storage room to take a phone call. Through the glass door, I can see her face bridge from happy to worry. I grab a towel to wipe my hands as I walk to stand by her.

"Okay, thanks for letting me know," Holly says as her eyes lock on mine as she disconnects the call.

"That was Beth," she says, looking perplexed. "Apparently, a social worker came by the inn, and when they went to the garden shed looking for me, she was not pleased with the living arrangements there, and Beth said she was writing notes in a notebook."

"Well, it's a good thing you're moving in here," I say

casually.

"Beau…"

"It's happening."

"Yeah, well, apparently, she's coming by here later today," she says worriedly.

I try to appear nonchalant for Holly. "Inconvenient, but it'll be fine."

"Yeah," she says, her voice full of worry. Her hand goes to her belly.

My fingers twine through hers, and I pull her into a hug. Each time I look at Holly, she seems to get even more beautiful.

"What did Beth say to her?" I ask.

"She told her she could find me here."

"Good. Then you should be all set."

"No, what if she doesn't like where I'm living and working, and she does something to take my baby from me? What if I'm not good enough?" she says with fear in her eyes.

"No one is taking our baby," I say protectively. "You'll be okay." I have this fierce desire to protect Holly and her baby, and I know that if this social worker has a problem with Holly, then she will have a problem with me, too. Now that she's here in my life, it's getting harder and harder to picture her out of it. Losing her and her baby would be worse right now than losing the restaurant.

I lean over and kiss her forehead. "Go take a break, and

it'll be okay. No matter what, just be relaxed and confident when you meet her."

She nods and heads upstairs. I get to work and make a plan for this woman.

I'm resetting the dining room for dinner when a middle-aged woman comes in with glasses perched on her nose. She looks like the older lady from the Disney movie *Monsters, Inc.* The one with the gravelly voice who told Mike Wazowski she was watching him. Then it clicks. She has to be the social worker. Of course, she would be.

"I'm looking for Holly Springs," she says pensively as she looks around, evaluating the space.

"Holly's upstairs resting right now. Can I help you?" I press.

"I need to speak with her if she's here," she says, taking a notebook and pen from her bag as she walks around and looks at things.

"I'll go get her," I say as I head to the stairs in the back to my apartment when I realize she's following me. "You can wait right out here, and I'll be right back."

She eyes me skeptically, and her eyes narrow, but she walks back into the dining room and waits.

"Hey, Hol, the social worker is here," I call calmly up the

stairs.

"Oh, okay, just a minute," she calls down in a cheerful voice. Good. She's doing what we rehearsed. Stay calm and confident.

She comes downstairs looking refreshed and relaxed after the short catnap I coaxed her into taking.

"Hey, sweetheart, I put your snack on the counter," I say as I pull her to me and tuck her into my side. "How was your nap?"

Her eyes widen as she stares at me, her back to the social worker. I've never called her that before, and I know she's nervous as hell. I hold her gaze, telling her with my eyes to just go with it.

She nods slightly and wraps her arms around me and kisses my cheek. "Thanks, honey."

We turn around, and I smile at the lady. "Sorry, this is…I didn't catch your name?"

"Betty Cranmore," she says as she looks back and forth between us skeptically. "I'm with the state of New Hampshire, and I'm here to do an evaluation on Holly. Is there somewhere we can talk privately, Holly?" She looks at me like she doesn't quite trust me, and that's okay because the feeling is mutual.

"Of course, right this way," I say, ignoring the fact that she just wants to talk to Holly and not me. I'm not leaving Holly to deal with this lady on her own. I don't trust her. I take them to a table in the dining room.

"What can I get you to drink?" I say as I get Holly settled.

She looks at the kitchen, then back at me, and she seems to be softening a little. "Oh, I guess that would be all right. A black coffee, please."

"Sure thing." I head back and get that for her and Holly's lunch and a glass of water. I set them down before them, and say, "Make sure you eat."

She nods, but her mouth turns up a little. "Thank you." I slide in next to Holly and lean back, tucking my arm around her.

The social worker watches us and writes a note in her notebook.

She sips her coffee and looks at me. "Thank you. And who are you to Holly?"

"I'm Beau, her partner," I say as Holly sips her water and coughs. "You okay?" I ask.

"Yes, just went down the wrong pipe," Holly says, shifting in her seat.

Betty's hand pauses over her notes, and I continue. "Holly and I live together and run the restaurant. Life partners," I state confidently.

"I see," she says.

"So you live here and work here?" she asks. "Not at the... shed that I visited?"

"No," Holly states. She doesn't break eye contact when

she says it, just like we talked about. "I live here."

"And will you be helping Holly with the baby?" She peers expectantly over at me over her glasses.

"Yes," I say.

"How long have you been together?" she asks.

"How is that relevant?" I ask. Holly squeezes my hand nervously.

"Just wondering," she murmurs as she gazes around the restaurant with a look I can't figure out.

"Have you been here before?" I wonder out loud to her.

She looks surprised. "Yes, this place used to be a special place for me."

I nod, curious and hoping she'll elaborate.

She continues to make notes but seems to relax a little more. "I'll need to see where you'll be living with the baby."

"Of course," Holly says softly, as she stares at the woman like she's trying to somehow place her.

"We can show you after Holly eats. She tries to keep to a schedule of her meals," I explain, trying to buy more time.

I'm sitting at the table facing Betty, and I can see the back of the restaurant where Evan and Ty have quietly come in and carried baby items upstairs while we've been sitting here keeping Betty busy. Holly doesn't know because she is sitting to the side of me and can't see the back door.

After Beth called Holly, Evan called and said he and Ty could bring over some of the twins' extra things to stage a nursery. I agreed and explained that I was having Holly move in anyway, and Evan and Beth agreed that would be a smart move with the social worker poking around.

"Would you like more coffee?" I offer.

"No, this is fine, thank you," she says with a tiny smile.

Ice is thawing.

"I can't place it," Holly says as she tilts her head. "But I know your name from somewhere."

Betty's eyes sadden, and she says, "My husband Tom and I used to get a pizza to go for years. It was our Friday tradition."

"That's right," Holly says, growing excited. "Extra pepperoni, cut in smaller slices."

Betty smiles, and her eyes dampen. "Yes."

"Why did you stop coming in? I haven't seen your Tom in here for over..." she says as realization sets in who the lady is.

"A year. My Tom passed away last year. I haven't gotten a pizza since." She sniffs.

I watch Holly's eyes fill, and she whispers, "Oh no, I'm so sorry, Betty. I didn't know he passed away. I looked forward to seeing him every Friday, and for a long time, I made his pizza at the same time hoping he'd come back, but he stopped coming, and I didn't know how to get ahold of him to figure out what happened."

Betty nods. "I miss him every day."

Holly reaches over and lays her hand on Betty's. "How about every Friday, you come in and eat pizza with us." She looks over at me, her face full of compassion.

"I couldn't do that," Betty objects. But something in her eyes looks like she has hope or happiness with this offer.

"Tom was so special to me," Holly says. "I always wondered why he stopped coming in. You guys don't live in Freedom Valley, do you?"

Betty softens. "No, we live a few towns over. But Freedom Pie is where he took me on my first date over forty years ago. I think right after it opened and your parents ran it. This was our special place. He'd always pick up our pizza every Friday after work and bring it home."

"Then you must keep coming. We insist. It is a special place. And we'd love to have you, wouldn't we, Beau?"

I nod. "Yes, of course." Even I'm starting to get emotional hearing Betty's story.

"I couldn't..." she protests, but I can tell on her face that Holly has just made her day with her kindness. I look over at Holly and realize this is part of who she is with Freedom Pie. This isn't just a family business. It's her community, and she really cares about everyone who comes in here.

"We'll see you this Friday," Holly says. Her face transforms as if she's forgotten this is a social worker who has her fate in her hands. She is in people-pizza mode and in her element, doing what she loves to do. I'm not sure of the exact moment when I started falling for Holly, but every day, I fall deeper and deeper.

"Well, that would be okay, I guess," she says as she looks in her purse for something.

Holly slides a pack of tissues over to her and smiles warmly at Betty.

I see Evan and Ty come back down the stairs and wave at me as they leave and quietly shut the back door.

"Well, let's go see the apartment," I say and stand.

"I'd love to see how you've set up for the baby," Betty says as she follows us.

Holly's eyes dart to me nervously.

We walk up the stairs into the apartment. The three-bedroom doors down the hall are all closed. She looks around and asks, "Where will the baby sleep?"

"I was going to..." Holly began nervously.

"Right here," I say as I open the door to the first bedroom that used to be Holly's.

Holly freezes in the doorway at the sight of diaper boxes stacked, a portable crib in the corner, and other baby items.

"We are excited to set up the nursery this weekend, aren't we?" I say to Holly, who is frozen in the doorway. I gently nudge her and put my arm around her shoulders.

"Yes. We sure are," she says, her hand covering her mouth as her eyes take everything in.

"The nursery always makes her so emotional. She's just

so excited," I explain to Betty as I take Holly's hand in mine and thread my fingers through hers and squeeze it gently.

I close the door and steer them both back to the living room. "Well, this is it."

"It's a lovely home," Betty says as she closes her notebook and tucks it away into her purse. "I'll have to check back in a few weeks, but everything seems to be great here."

"But we'll see you Friday, right?" Holly asks hopefully.

"I'd like that," Betty whispers.

We head back down, and Betty leaves. As soon as the door jingles and shuts, Holly looks at me. "Where did all that stuff come from?"

"Evan wanted to drop some stuff by. While we sat at the table, he and Ty snuck it all up there."

She throws her head back and laughs before locking eyes with me, and her lips reach mine like magnets, not able to stay apart. She looks at me and says, "Amazing. You are amazing, Beau. You don't have to do all of this, you know that, right?"

I shrug. "I want to."

Her eyes shine as we clean the kitchen with soft music in the background. She's cutting up vegetables, and I come up behind her, put my hands on her belly, and pull her back against me. I lean down and kiss her cheek.

"I got you, Holly," I whisper.

She sucks in a breath and relaxes against me.

That night, we made a trip to the inn and grabbed the last of Holly's things so she's officially living at the apartment now. She didn't have a lot, but we got all her things just in time for the snow to start coming down heavy again.

"I'm glad I don't have to drive back and forth in this anymore." She laments as she follows me in from the truck.

"Me, too," I say as I carry her bags upstairs, and she follows me.

"I'm going to go take a shower and put on pajamas," she says.

"Of course. I'll close up downstairs and make us a snack."

"You're always feeding me." She laughs.

"Maybe I'm hungry, too," I scoff.

I'm lying on the couch with a bowl of popcorn and a blanket when she comes out of the bedroom and stands in the doorway. I pull the blanket up and motion for her to scoot in beside me. She slides in next to me and gets cozy.

"I thought we could watch a movie together," I say.

"What do you want to watch?"

"Something funny." She shrugs, taking a handful of popcorn.

"We could binge-watch every Adam Sandler movie," I offer.

"Deal," she says.

She leans against me and ends up falling asleep with her head on my chest. My fingers trail up and down her arms, the rest of her skin soothing and tantalizing to the touch. I feel like I've been with Holly for a lifetime in the best way possible. Like she's always been here for me all along. We only make it through half the movie. I carry her to bed and tuck her in on the opposite side of mine. I clean and head to bed. My heart feels so grateful having her here. I love being around her. She lies with her back to me, and I want to hold her. She mumbles and scoots toward me, and I settle my arm around her, resting my hand on her stomach. She sighs deeply, and her body relaxes next to mine.

All feels right with her here.

CHAPTER 21

Holly

"What are you two listening to?" Hank pops in the doorway to the kitchen as he watches Beau and I cook.

"I'm introducing your brother to Taylor Swift. He's a Swiftie now," I say as I sprinkle ham on top of a pizza.

Beau shakes his head and mumbles defiantly, "No, I am not."

I point at him, feigning disappointment. "You've been humming along."

"That's because you've been torturing me by making me listen to every single Taylor Swift album for two days now." He holds up his hands covered in dough. "It's all I have."

"What's your favorite album?" Hank asks.

"*Folklore*," I say.

"I'm more of a *Red* type of guy," Hank says with a smile as he snags a pile of pepperoni and eats it.

"I had no idea you were a Swiftie," I say as I quickly dice up peppers for prep.

"So are you two like really a couple? Like for real?" Hank changes the subject as he looks between us.

Beau's eyes cut to mine to see my reaction as I smile nervously. "Yes," I say as I look at Beau, but it comes out more like a question.

"Yes," Beau confirms. "If anyone asks, you say yes. Especially that nosy social worker."

"She was really sweet. I think she's just sad and lonely. I'm looking forward to her coming in on Friday."

"She is nice, but if she messes things up for you, she's never getting pizza here again."

"I thought we were pretending," I whisper as my eyes close, hopeful for what I want him to say next.

"I know what I said, but I don't want to pretend anymore. I changed my mind." And then his mouth lands on mine. Suddenly, I am no longer as confused about Beau. He wants me, and I want him.

"Hey, get a room!" Hank teases, reminding us that he's here, too. "Also, can I get one of those to go?" He eyes the pizza.

"All meat?" Beau replies, smiling.

"You know it, brother. I'm happy for you guys. I've always wanted to be an uncle, and I'll teach the baby everything I know."

"Which won't be much." Beau scoffs. "You're not corrupting this baby."

I'm just happy that they're lightening the mood after that confirmation. A smile spreads across my face when I picture Beau and Hank with the baby. I always wanted to have a big family, but it was only me and my parents and the rest of the town if you count them. This is why community is so important to me. I watch Hank and Beau with their friendly teasing and imagine what it must have been like for them as teenagers losing their parents and finding their way together.

"I stopped by because it's going to get really bad out there. We're putting out warnings to everyone in town. Stock up on supplies. We're supposed to get the snowstorm of the century," Hank adds.

"I heard that, too. I need to run next door and grab some supplies from the general store," Beau says.

"Whatever you get, grab extra just in case I need some." Hank grins.

Beau playfully rolls his eyes as he finishes making Hank's pizza and slides it into the oven. "Watch this and take this out when it's done. Holly will tell you when. It's heavy, so don't let her do it," Beau says, looking at me with a warning look. He's always trying to keep me from lifting too much. I give him a mock salute and continue prepping.

"I'll just be next door. You need anything, Holly?" Beau asks as he slides on his black Carhartt coat and waits for me to respond.

Hank says, "Get me some Twizzlers, will you?"

"I'm good," I admit.

"You eat like a five-year-old," he tells Hank.

"I know you are, but what am I?" Hank says in a mocking voice.

"Real mature," Beau says, but he's smiling. "Be back." He kisses me quickly, heads out, and shuts the door.

Hank slides up on a stool beside me and pleads, "Don't let me burn that pizza. He'll kill me."

I laugh. "Okay, I'll tell you when to take it out. But I can do it," I say.

"Not a chance, I'll get it. So what are your intentions with my brother?" Hank asks as he grabs a piece of pepper and eats it. "I really like him." I bite my lip as I smile. "Like a lot."

"Me, too," Hank says. "So don't hurt him. He already had one woman do a number on him."

"I won't." I can't imagine hurting Beau. He's the kind of guy who would give you his shirt right off his back and walk through fire for the people he loves. I will never understand why his ex didn't see what I see.

He stops scrolling and looks over at me. "I mean it. He's a

tough guy, but he's soft under that hard exterior."

"I promise. Although I don't understand why she could do that to him."

"Me either. Someone who destroys your mental health cannot be the love of your life," he says as he shakes his head.

"I'm glad he's away from her, then." I frown.

"She's a terrible person. Satan's preparing her bedroom as we speak."

I laugh but then turn to him and say, "I just don't want him to think he has to take care of me and my baby. I can take care of us, but I do really like Beau. So much."

Hank frowns. "He really likes you, too. And it's not about obligation. If he's here, it's because he wants to be. He'll always do the right thing, but he has always known exactly what he wants and gone after that."

"Do you think he'd like me if I wasn't pregnant?"

"Why, are you regretting doing the surrogacy?"

"No, I think things turned out like they did for a reason. Not the way I would have exactly planned it, but look how it's turning out."

"This place was worth fighting for," he says, looking around. "It's a great restaurant. Your family did good with it."

"Thanks, this has been pretty much the only home I've ever known," I say as I check the pizza. "It's done if you want to take it out."

He grabs the wooden pan and slides it into the wood oven and pulls out the pizza. "Perfection," he says proudly, laying it on the board to cut.

"Show me how to cut this thing?" Hank asks as he tries to figure out how to cut the pizza.

"Like this," I say as I cut the pizza and slide it into the box.

He picks up a slice and bites into it. "Holly, you are a miracle worker. I could eat this every single day. Thank God you saved Beau from the shit pizza he was making."

"Hey, I heard that," Beau says, coming in the back door with his arms full of bags.

Hank walks over and takes some of the bags. "It's true, and you know it."

I take a few of the bags from Beau and start to unpack them. "Those go upstairs," he says.

"How was it out there?" I ask.

"Pretty bad. We're definitely not driving anywhere, and I doubt we will get many customers tonight. They're closing early next door, and I think we'd better close early, too."

"I'm on shift, so please don't go anywhere. We don't want any accidents." Hank shudders and shakes his head.

"Stay warm!" I call as he slides on his coat and picks up his pizza box.

"Will do, Mom!" He grins as he waves and shuts the door.

Mom.

I'm going to be a mom. I'm still wrapping my head around this. Seeing the nursery items in my old bedroom made all this even more real. I mentally run through my list of all that I need to do and things that I need to buy. Overwhelm sets in. Most expectant mothers have nine months to prepare. I just have a few weeks.

CHAPTER 22

Beau

"I guess we picked a good time for me to move in here," she says as she leans back against the counter and looks out the window at all the snow.

"No kidding. Why don't you sit down and keep me company?" I nod to her. She's been on her feet for a long time.

"Hank says they'll probably be responding to a lot of calls," she says, looking worried.

"Yeah, I imagine they will be busy. We could make up a bunch of pizzas and have them ready for the first responders," I say as I glance at our supplies in the cooler. "We're low on boxes, though. We won't get our shipment in until Friday."

"I have plenty of black market boxes," she says sheepishly.

I grin and shake my head. "Of course you do. Where are they?"

"Over at Allie's in the bakery," she says as she reaches for her phone to text Allie.

"I'll text Hank and let him know," I say as I pull out my phone and fire off a text to him.

Me: Holly and I can make pizzas for the firefighters and paramedics today or tomorrow. Whatever works. I know you will probably be busy.

Hank: Thanks! I'll let them know. There are six of us on shift tonight.

Me: Okay, we'll get you taken care of.

Holly looks over at me with a worried look on her face. "I worry about some of our older people in town. The people who might not have enough wood for heat or groceries."

"We could make pizzas for the first responders to drop off to the people without food. Let's see how many extra pizzas we can make."

"You'll do that?" Holly says, her eyes getting misty.

"Of course I will. We can't let people go hungry," I say, getting more dough out.

I stop and turn to look at her, and she smiles at me. "What?"

"Careful, Beau, this town will start to fall in love with you."

I don't need the whole town to fall in love with me. Just you.

"We'll tell everyone it was your idea. I have an asshole reputation to uphold," I tease.

She scoffs. "No one would believe you're an asshole if they really knew you."

"You did." I laugh.

"Well, now that I know you, I know that's not true," she says quietly. Her phone goes off, and she tips it up to read a notification.

"Allie has the boxes, and Logan will drop them off when he picks her up. Her car won't make it out of the bakery parking lot. Think we could make a pizza for them?" she says as she stirs sauce on the stove.

"What kind do they like?"

"Sausage and mushroom," she says automatically.

I laugh. "Do you know everyone's pizza orders?"

She shrugs. "Pretty much. Oh, hey, can you check on Stephen? My dad would bring his little house in when we got really bad weather."

I pause, waiting to see if she's messing with me.

She looks over. "What?"

My eyes widen, and I stare. "Wait, you're serious?"

"Yes, he'll freeze out there, and his house gets snow-packed, and he can't get in or out," she says worriedly.

"What if he bites me?" I scoff.

"He won't bite you. This is Stephen we're talking about." She looks at me like I'm the crazy one for being leery about bringing a wild squirrel into the restaurant.

"Okay, maybe he won't bite me, but what's he going to do in the restaurant?" I protest.

"What do you mean?" she asks, confused.

"*Holly*. This is a wild animal."

She lays the wooden spoon across the top of the sauce pot and comes around to face me. "This is Stephen. He's lived here for several years now and never caused a problem. In fact, he already comes and goes as he pleases. But we need to bring his house in to keep it safe and dry for him. He knows the drill and that it's temporary."

"He knows it's temporary," I repeat. "What in the world? He's a squirrel! How does he know that?"

She shrugs. "Because he's Stephen." She turns and walks to the back door, grabbing her coat.

"What are you doing?" I call.

"Going to get his house."

"No, you're not!" I grab a towel, wipe my hands, and follow her. I step in front of her and hold up my hands, breathing out a sigh of defeat. "I will get him."

Holly tilts her head at me like she's waiting for me to make a break for it and not really do it.

I take a deep breath and brace myself. I reach up to get

his house, and my hand brushes fur. I squeal and jump. "He touched me! He touched me!"

Holly is doubled over laughing so hard.

"Not funny."

"No, you're right," she wheezes. "That was hilarious."

I stare at her with disdain. "I'm so glad you think so."

She shivers. "Hurry, it's cold out here."

I take a deep breath and nod. *I can do this*, I tell myself, trying to amp myself up.

"You know, for a big bad former military man, you sure are scared of a little fuzzy squirrel." She grins as she folds her arms, shivering.

I shake my head. "Not true. I'm not scared."

Her eyebrows raise. "You squealed."

"I don't know what you're talking about," I clip as I reach up and carefully unhook his little gazebo house and pull it down as he scurries out of it.

"Come on, buddy!" Holly calls to him.

Stephen climbs down and runs in the back door, and I look at her and say, "If the health department comes, we're done for."

She looks at me and smirks. "The health department isn't coming out in this weather, and it's just until the storm passes. We can set him up in the dining room in the corner."

"Will he get into anything?" I ask as I run a hand over my face.

"No. He's a good boy, aren't you, Stephen?" she says. "But you have to make him his own personal pizza."

"What?" I ask in disbelief.

"Gotcha," she says, laughing again.

With a shake of my head, I chase her back into the kitchen and grab her and tickle her.

"Okay, okay." She laughs.

I reach down and kiss her softly, pulling her to me, my hands holding her face and her hands gripping my waist. We hear someone clear their throat and look over to see Allie and Logan holding a large stack of unfolded pizza boxes.

"Oh, hi," Holly says as she grins and waves.

"Hi." Allie smirks as she looks back and forth between us.

Logan holds up the boxes. "Where should I put these?"

"I'll take them," I say as I reach for them and stack them in the storage room.

"So you and pizza brother?" Allie says quietly to Holly.

Holly nervously laughs. "Yeah. Oh! Hey, we made you something," she says as she hands them the sausage and mushroom pizza.

"Thank you, that smells great," Logan says. "And we're starving, too."

"Yes, thank you. We have to get home before the roads get worse. You guys have everything you need?" Allie asks. "Oh, and I made *you* something." She hands Holly a pan of cinnamon rolls.

"Allie, thank you! You're the best!" Holly looks up at the ceiling with delight.

Allie looks at her and mouths. "Call me and tell me everything."

Holly just grins and clutches the pan of cinnamon rolls to her chest.

"I hear this is supposed to be the snowstorm of the century," Logan says.

"So I've heard as well. Stay safe," I call and wave as they head out.

The door closes, and I grin at Holly. She shakes her head and wraps a hand around my waist.

I look nervously out to the dining room and see Stephen asleep on a towel in his little house, with his tail hanging out the gazebo window. I shake my head. When I signed up for the restaurant, I didn't realize it came with a pet squirrel. My new life is a strange one. I look over at Holly and grin, but it's good.

CHAPTER 23

Beau

We close up the restaurant, and Holly heads upstairs to shower and get in comfy clothes while I scoop snow for what feels like the five hundredth time today and wait for the fire truck to come and get their order. I want to keep up with it, but it seems never-ending. We already have five-foot drifts in front of the restaurant, but I have kept shoveling. Growing up in Vermont, I know the snowstorm game. But this storm is a big one.

I hear honking and look up to see the fire truck following the snowplow as it pulls up in front on Main Street. The fire truck has a festive winter wreath on the front of it, and Hank leans out and waves.

"Hey, loser, where's our pizza?" he teases from the truck window and grins as he jumps down.

"Inside, let me grab them." I set the shovel against the building as I watch my little brother stand beside the fire truck. Watching him fulfill his dream of carrying on our dad's legacy of becoming a firefighter has been worth every sacrifice. My chest swells with pride for him.

"Come on, Lawson," Hank calls as another guy slides down from the truck.

"We made you a bunch of different ones. Sardines for you, asshole," I joke as he claps me on the back, and we walk to the kitchen.

"I'm so hungry I would literally eat sardine pizza right now." He shakes his head.

"I made you double meat lovers like you asked. Holly packed up a few desserts as well."

"Where is your little momma?" he asks as he looks around.

"Upstairs for the night. Trying to get her to take it easy."

He nods. "Good. Don't let her go into labor during this storm. I'm not delivering any babies."

I scoff. "She's not going into labor anytime soon, and you will not be delivering her baby."

We get all the food loaded, and I wave as they push through the big snow drifts and make their way down the street to the fire station. After I lock up, I finish cleaning and fold boxes for tomorrow. The lights flicker, and the power goes off. I had already anticipated this happening and set up the gas generator for heat in the apartment. No way am I not keeping Holly and the baby warm. I keep the wood-fired oven going to keep the restaurant warm and tested that the heat rises to the apartment. We should be good to go.

As I work, I think about how my life has changed and how I ended up here. And while I'm not sure how, I'm grateful I ended up here.

When our parents died, I had a steady girlfriend during my senior year of high school. When I assumed responsibility for Beau, she went to college, and I worked full time until I joined. We didn't have much in common after that. In the military, I had a few relationships, but none that were serious. I was busy with training, work, and Beau. He was a good kid, but he was still a kid, and he kept me on my toes, parenting him when I was still a kid myself. I had no time for relationships and couldn't give them the time they deserved. I've always known what I wanted in a relationship and been okay with being single. With Holly, I want everything with her. Even her damn squirrel.

I look over the dark restaurant and scrub my hand over my face. I nod in satisfaction. This has always been my dream, and here I have it and more. More than I could ever have expected when I moved to Freedom Valley.

When Hank graduated from firefighter school, I came back for his graduation and met my ex Nadia. She was drop-dead gorgeous, driven, and ambitious. When she told me later that she was pregnant, I was over the moon with excitement. I've always wanted to be a dad and have a family. Sure, it was a surprise, but I rolled with it. Hank was less than thrilled because he'd never liked Nadia, and now, looking back, I think he saw things I didn't. Red flags, things you don't see when you think you're head over heels in love with someone and overlook their flaws. And surprisingly, I did. Nadia played me, and she played me good.

Nadia didn't want to be an Army wife, and she made it very clear she didn't want to move away from Vermont. I didn't want to be away from Nadia and our baby. So I gave up my military career and moved back to Vermont to marry Nadia and become a dad. Only when I got there, she told me that she'd lost the baby. We still got married despite Hank trying to tell me not to.

We opened our own restaurant and poured our energy into that despite the sadness of losing the baby. After two years, I realized that things with Nadia were never what I thought they were. One night when she was working late, I surprised her at the restaurant by showing up and found her having sex with one of our cooks on the kitchen prep counter. And this had been going on for a while with a lot of our staff.

And to make matters worse, a few weeks after that, she got drunk one night and admitted she was never pregnant and she had been cheating on me throughout our entire marriage. Everything with Nadia was a lie.

I mourned the loss of a baby that had never existed. And I had always wondered why Nadia didn't seem to be as sad as I was. Because she got what she wanted. I was out of the military, with her, and helping her open her restaurant. I worked tirelessly for years, and in the end, she had screwed me over by putting everything mostly in her name and barely paying me a salary. She'd say that we were working to get the restaurant up and running, and it would be in the black soon. "Soon" was always what I heard. Only there was never a soon. She kept me working long hours at the restaurant so she could go and screw every guy she could and lie to me constantly.

When I walked away from our marriage, I walked away with less than I came in with. I have a tough time trusting anyone after that. Yet here I am, letting Holly in. And I can't even explain why. But I really like her, and dare I even admit, I'm falling for her. She's everything I've ever wanted. A woman I love being with and will have a family with. And the restaurant? Just another thing we're both passionate about. Life with Holly is easy and fun. We laugh a lot, we eat together, we even sleep together. Not sex, just sleep. I love being with her and want to be with her every minute I'm awake. I want to know what her dreams are, and I want to help her make them happen. I want to know her baby and help her. I want this. Goddamn, I want this so bad.

I look at my watch, and it's still only seven thirty, so I head to the kitchen to make a snack. Lately, Holly has had a sweet tooth this time of night, and it's usually chocolate. I scrounge around the kitchen to see what I can surprise her with and make us both s'mores cups. I arrange everything on a tray and carry it up the back steps. I step into the apartment, and she's on the phone with who I'm guessing is Ophelia.

"No way. Your power is out, too? Same," she says as she's stretched out on the couch, her hand over her belly.

"Have you talked to Hank today?" She listens, and her eyes widen as she sees me. "Hey, let me text you later. Beau is here, and he brought dessert." She listens, and her face reddens, and she grins. "No, I'm not telling him that. Bye, Opi," she says as she disconnects.

"Tell me what?" I ask, setting the tray down. I pick up her feet and sit, placing them on my lap.

She grins and looks at the s'mores and back at me. "How did you know I was craving chocolate?"

I eye her and smile. "You're always craving chocolate," I say as I rub her feet.

She puts her head back and groans with pleasure. "Please keep doing that," she murmurs.

She's beautiful and sexy, I think as I watch her face.

"Why do you have to be so perfect?" She moans.

"I'm far from perfect. I just know what you need."

Her eyes darken. "You have no idea what I need."

"What do you need?" I ask as I rub her feet, not breaking eye contact.

She takes a deep breath, and her breath hitches. Her face is unreadable, but she seems to be deep in thought.

"Baby okay?" I ask softly.

She nods. "Yeah, all good."

"What's wrong?" I ask softly. I hope she's not having second thoughts. Being with Holly has made me happy, and I don't want to lose what I have with her. There's too much at stake now.

She sits up and tucks her feet under her, moving next to me.

She looks at me and finally says, "I like what we have."

I tilt my head and take her hand in mine. "Why do I feel like there's a 'but'?"

"My ears hear what you've said, but my head keeps telling my heart not to get attached to this idea of 'us.' I know it has to be frustrating, I want to trust that all of this will work, and I think it will take some time until my brain stops whispering doubts to me."

"We're doing us, Hol," I say, locking eyes with her. "And sometimes that just looks like us. Not what everyone else has, just us. You and me and our baby. We're here, now, and together. I like us. We have everything we need."

"What if me and the baby are too much?" she whispers nervously.

"What do you mean too much?"

"I'm having a baby, and that baby will change everything," she says as she twists a lock of her hair.

"It'll change everything for me, too," I agree. And it will. Because babies change everything. And this one is going to be for the good.

"What do you mean?" she asks, stilling and looking at me.

"That's our baby now," I claim.

Her eyes seem to melt as she looks at me. I pull her to me and gather her close. "I meant what I said. You and me and our baby."

"Okay," she says softly. "It's just a lot, you know. And I want to make sure you're still good with everything."

"Are you good with everything?" I ask, hoping she's not having second thoughts.

"I am good with us. Just overwhelmed with everything that I have to do. I haven't even thought about names. I need to buy things..." She covers her face with her hands and sighs.

"Hey, I'll help you. We'll make a list and divide and conquer, right?" I say, stroking her cheek.

"Yeah, you're right. Thank you, Beau," she says as her body relaxes into mine.

"We'll be alright."

CHAPTER 24

Holly

I wake up from a dream and stretch, feeling warmth all around me. I'm lying with Beau's arms wrapped around me and my belly, holding us protectively. The feeling of waking up from a dream to it being my reality is still not something I'm used to.

I think about what he said to me last night. *That's my baby now.*

He wants not only me but also this baby. How my life can go from trying to get the restaurant back from this man and doing everything possible to do that, even getting pregnant as a surrogate for money to do that, and then finding myself a single mom with said man telling me that's his baby now.

What is my life right now?

I don't know, but I love it. Somehow this shit show has turned into a dream life.

Standing, I reach for my robe and tie it tight, then walk to the window to look down at Main Street. All I see is white and lots of it. No street, sidewalks, or cars in sight. I've rarely seen Main Street this quiet with no people or sounds.

"Hey." Beau stretches, then comes to stand behind me, putting his arms around me. He leans down and kisses my neck, rubbing my belly. "How did you sleep?"

"Really good, you?" I murmur, leaning into him.

"I always sleep good when you're here," he says.

"Looks like the power's still out," I say.

"Yeah, it doesn't look like it's letting up either," he says as he looks through the blinds.

"At least the kitchen runs on gas." I shrug. "We can still cook."

"That we can," he mutters. "We can make pizzas for the locals without power if you want."

"Yes, I was thinking that too. I'm honestly glad we're snowed in. We can relax. I was supposed to have my ultrasound today. Obviously, that's not happening now," I murmur.

He picks up my hand and twines my fingers in his. "I want to come. When you reschedule, that is."

"You do?"

"I told you that's my baby now," he says as he looks at me with nothing but desire. And it makes my toes curl. I close my eyes and lean my head against his chest.

"How do you feel about that?" he asks.

"It feels good. But scary. All of this is scary and new," I admit.

"I'm not scared," he declares. "I've always wanted to be a dad, more than anything."

"Really?" I ask. "I mean, I'm not really surprised. You pretty much raised Hank. You did a great job. He's a great guy."

"We raised each other. We were so young, but we made it. I'd like to think I'll be a good dad," he says as he pulls on a hooded sweatshirt, his hair disheveled and sexy. Damn, he's a good-looking man.

"You'll be a great dad," I say as desire fills me just looking at him. "What are you doing?"

"Going to make us breakfast and coffee. You want a decaf coffee?"

"I want a full caf. But yeah, I will take what I can get." I grin.

"Soon. You don't have that much longer," he says. "Hey, when you do your ultrasound, will you find out the gender?"

"I was thinking of being surprised," I admit. "What do you think since you want to be the dad and all?" I tease.

"I think whatever you want, we'll do," he says as he slides

on his shoes, leans down to tie them, and looks back up at me. How he manages to make tying his shoes look sexy, I'll never understand.

I nod. Being snowed in with sexy Beau is going to be *fun*.

I get dressed and head downstairs to find Beau making eggs on the stove, pouring a mug of coffee, and taking a sip. He looks relaxed and at home here in the kitchen. A year ago when it was just me running the kitchen with my parents here helping out a few days a week, I never could have imagined where we'd all be today.

I have to tell my parents. And soon. How do I tell them that I got pregnant with a surrogate's baby, and now I'm keeping said baby, and oh yeah, I'm shacking up with one of the guys who bought your restaurant. They already seemed disappointed with me when they moved to Florida, and I didn't move with them. Things have been tense since they sold the restaurant. I mean, I get why they did it, but I still don't like it. I want it back. And in a way I couldn't have even begun to have orchestrated. And I got Beau. And he's the most unexpected, best thing that has ever happened to me. Because it's our baby now.

I watch as he casually makes eggs and toast for us, his hair still disheveled and his hoodie on. This man could be mine.

He wants me. He wants us.

I've dated on and off but never found anyone I wanted to be serious with. My parents married young and had me later in life. A surprise baby in their mid-forties didn't seem like a great surprise, but they never treated me like they didn't want me. I had an idyllic childhood growing up here at Freedom Pie. Sure, I was in the kitchen making pizza as soon as my hands could reach the counter and rolling pin, but this place made me who I am.

Living here with Beau is scary. It's not mine. It's all his. And at any time, all of this could end. He stops wanting to play house with me if that's all this is. What happens when the snowstorm honeymoon, so to speak, wears off, and he finds out a screaming newborn in his space is not what he wants after all? Where does that leave us? No place to live, work, or Beau. And I'm starting to fall for him. Hard. And I don't know that I could take it if I give him my whole heart and trust and then end up losing it. We're still so new. But he seems confident in what he wants. Me and the baby.

I can risk it all and try with him or play it safe and guard my heart. But it feels like with every wall I put up with Beau, he simultaneously dismantles and stacks them aside. He's methodical in his love and care for me and clearly wants me. And the feeling is one hundred percent mutual. I want Beau so badly my heart aches.

When he touches me, holds my hand, or simply lays a

hand on my lower back when we're cooking, my heart melts more and more with every day that goes by.

"I see you up there," he calls, breaking my daydreaming.

"I see you down there," I call back, stepping down the last few steps and smiling at him as he hands me a warm mug of coffee with vanilla creamer just like I like it.

"Decaf for you, my lady," he says as he slides eggs onto plates from the skillet.

"What are we going to do today?" I ask as I take the plate he hands me, and we carry our coffee and plates to the dining room.

"Let's sit by the window and watch the snow," he says as he walks to the other side of the restaurant, farther from our usual booth by the kitchen.

"Good idea," I say as I set my dishes down and slide into the booth across from him.

"I texted Hank, and he's on shift again today. He said there are a lot of hungry people out there, and the fire department is willing to play Santa and deliver pizzas in the truck if we have any to give."

"Let's do it. Do we have enough supplies?"

He nods at me over his coffee. "Yes, we can do that. I'll put some of your Christmas movies on down here, and I want you to rest, though. Being on your feet so much is not good for you."

"Yes, Dad," I say with a smile as I roll my eyes. But when I look at him, he's looking at me very seriously. "What?"

He shakes his head and grins. "Nothing. Joking or not, I like that. I told you that I want to be a dad."

I don't say anything, but my heart swells in my chest, making me feel warm.

"Still scared?" he asks as he forks eggs and eats them, tilting his head as he waits for me to answer.

I nod. "If we don't work, what happens? Where do I go? I wouldn't have a job, home, or you. And I really, really like you, Beau," I whisper, a lump forming in my throat.

His eyes soften, and he slides out of his booth and over into mine, reaching for his plate and mug.

He looks over at me. "I don't leave, Holly. It's not who I am. And it's not you either. This?" he says as he looks around the restaurant. "This is ours. We can build a life together here. I have no idea how life worked this all out for us, but what a life it will be. You, me, our baby, and this restaurant. Another generation here building a life. Do you want that?"

I nod. "Having a family here is all I've ever wanted." Excitement fills me for our future. I'm in deep now. Beau has my heart in his hands, and I'm a goner. He's everything I never knew I needed. The most unexpected love that leaves me emotional and brimming with joy.

"Then let's do it, Holly. Let's build a life together."

CHAPTER 25

Beau

"Are you excited?" I ask her as I slide my hand into her gloved hand and pull her closer as we trudge through the snow piles and into the clinic.

"Yes, are you?" she says.

I nod. "I get to see the baby and spend the morning with you. Of course I'm excited."

"How do you think Hank is doing at the shop?" she asks.

I shudder and close my eyes for a second. "I don't want to know. Last time, he almost burned the place down."

"Hopefully, Ophelia won't let him start any fires. And hey, if he does, at least he's a firefighter and can put the fire out." She laughs.

I snort laugh as I hold the door, and Holly passes through. I stand with her while she checks in and notice other couples in the waiting room together. I'm glad Holly let me come with her to her appointment. I wouldn't have wanted her to be alone, and I really want to be here with her. I don't want to miss anything.

We take a seat, and I think about us together at the hospital when it's time. Then bringing the baby home together and making a home together above the restaurant. A fridge with kid's artwork on it. Our baby raised in the restaurant just like Holly was. Family dinners and traditions that we make together. Life with Holly and the baby.

I put my hand around her and pull her to me protectively. *My family.*

"You okay?" she asks as she leans up to look at me.

"Yes," I say as I lean my face down and kiss her softly.

"Holly?" someone says from the doorway, and we both look up to see the nurse.

We step into the room, and the nurse says cheerfully, "How are you doing, Mom and Dad?"

I say nothing, still nervous as hell being here with her, and luckily, Holly interjects. "We are good," she says, looking at me, and doesn't correct the nurse about me not being the father. Maybe she's finally understanding that I'm all in.

The ultrasound technician comes in, and honestly, I couldn't tell you what she said. I was glued to the ultrasound screen when she panned over the baby and mentioned the arms, fingers, and toes. She then took pictures and printed them out. I held Holly's hand and sat with her, feeling a tidal wave of emotions I never expected to feel.

Holly hands me the photos of the baby, and I can't believe how emotional I'm getting over black-and-white photos of a baby we haven't even held.

"Baby is measuring at approximately thirty-six weeks. Looks like you have a healthy baby," she says as she cleans up the equipment and wipes Holly's belly with a towel.

I squeeze Holly's hand, and she squeezes back, her eyes misty as she looks at mine.

Holly asks a few questions, and I send the pictures to Hank in a text message.

> **Hank:** You got it bad, bro. I'm happy for you. You deserve this with Holly. Don't let what happened with Nadia ruin this experience for you.
>
> **Me:** Thanks. I'm trying not to.
>
> **Hank:** Guess what?
>
> **Me:** If you burned my kitchen down, I'm going to kill you.
>
> **Hank:** (Eye roll emoji) I did not burn your kitchen down this time. But there's always next time.
>
> **Me:** What then?
>
> **Hank:** Ophelia and I are officially dating. We're not moving as fast as you and Holly making a family, but I think Opi could be the one.

I smile upon hearing this. I love that Hank is happy here in Freedom Valley. We're both finding happy here.

Me: I'm happy for you. We'll be back soon.

As long as Holly wants me, I will be hers.

A dark thought passes through me, and I think about what would happen if Holly were to leave. What if she decides to go to Florida with the baby to be closer to her family? What if they leave me? I've lost everything before, and I could lose it all again. My breath almost leaves my chest with the thought. I've grown used to having Holly with me for the past month, and she's become my world. We've spent nearly every moment together, and I don't want to lose what we have. Whatever we have, I want it. All of it. The good, the bad, and the complicated. This love is what I want.

After we return, Holly takes a nap upstairs, leaving me with my thoughts, and it's not good. I'm starting to panic, thinking about losing all of this again. Well, I never actually had any of this the first time. But now? Now, the stakes are higher. I'm in deep. Hank was right.

Hank comes in from taking out the trash and is covered in snow. He glances over at me and then back quickly. "You good?"

I shake my head and pace the kitchen, my hands on my hips. "No."

He looks up at the apartment. "Is it Holly?"

I nod. "I really, really like her. More than just like...I love her," I confess in a whisper. "I know it's been quick, but sometimes you just know. Am I crazy?"

Hank's mouth turns up, and he grins.

"Don't answer that." I glare.

Hank relaxes his shoulders. "This is different. Last time with Nadia, she did a number on you. I hated Nadia, you know that. Holly's...different. She's special. And the difference in Holly and Nadia is that I don't think Nadia ever loved you, and I'm sorry to tell you that. But Holly looks at you like you don't just light up the room. No, you power the whole fucking sun for Holly. She has it just as bad for you as you do for her."

"You really think so?" I say, letting out a deep breath.

"You two are as sickeningly sweet as a Taylor Swift song. You're like a match that doesn't make sense, but it does." He shrugs.

"Which Taylor Swift song?" I question.

Hank swivels around, triumphantly laughing as he points. "I knew it! I knew you secretly liked it when she made you listen to all those Taylor Swift albums."

I shrug, pretending not to really care, and mutter, "I just asked what song."

"Ask Holly," he grins. "Listen, this Friday at the inn, Evan is having a get-together. They made igloos by the firepit out of these tent things that are freaking awesome. I reserved one for you and Holly. We're playing games and hot chocolate and all that stuff. Bring Holly at seven."

We've spent so much time here at the restaurant it would be nice to take her out and do stuff together, especially before the baby comes. "Yeah, okay, I'll talk to her and see if she wants to do that."

He looks at me. "Oh, she wants to. She and Opi have been discussing it all day, hoping you'll ask her. She doesn't think you'll want to go."

"Why would she think that?" I grump.

"Oh, I don't know," he says sarcastically. "Maybe because you're a grumpy introverted asshole who never goes anywhere. And she *still* fell for you."

I playfully punch his shoulder.

"Alright, I need to go do some work on my house. You got this?" Hank says, pushing off the counter.

"Yeah, thanks for your help."

"Don't mess anything up with Holly. She's perfect for you."

Beau

"Thanks for your help," Evan says as we finish putting the last of the igloos together on the back property of the inn.

"Sure, anytime. Thanks for doing CPR on my restaurant and helping me get my customers back," I say as I snap the last piece of the igloo together. The black PVC pipe and plastic tops make them look like strong, clear giant umbrellas perfect for stargazing and fun family nights under the dark, starry sky. Each igloo holds approximately eight people and has been set up with chairs, blankets, board games, and pillows. A coffee and hot cocoa bar has been set up in the middle of an old, rehabbed shed so people can enjoy warm beverages.

"Nah, you had it. You just needed to add in Holly's magic. Now you're a dynamic duo. She was a missing piece of the puzzle for you. It's amazing how that's all worked out or is working out," he says as his eyes meet mine.

"It is working out," I say as I see Holly holding one of Evan and Beth's babies. She's cooing and making the baby laugh as it reaches for Holly's face with chubby little baby hands.

"She's going to make a great mom," I murmur. Holly smiles and throws her head back, laughing at something Beth says to her. She's compassionate, protective, and fierce. I couldn't have picked a stronger woman to be with. She's the woman I always wanted. And it's funny how life works and doesn't work out sometimes.

"And you'll make a great dad," Evan says as he stands back and watches Beth and Holly too.

"I have no idea how to be a dad," I admit.

"I didn't either, and I got twins to break me in. You'll be fine," Evan says with a chuckle.

"When my parents died, I finished raising Hank. I didn't know what I was doing there either. But I figure he didn't turn out too bad," I say as I look over at Hank making a fire in the firepit off to the side, talking to Ophelia.

"Hank's a great guy. Ophelia seems really happy. You did good," Evan says as Pete the handyman walks up to us carrying baskets in both hands.

"Hey, Pete, got the food?" Evan asks.

"Sasha made soup, sandwiches, and desserts for the igloo renters," Pete says as he hands one to me.

"Thanks, that sounds great. I wanted to surprise Holly. I think she'll like it," I say, tucking it under my arm.

I look over, and Holly's eyes are on mine. She tips her head at the picnic basket and looks at me questioningly. I motion to her to come this way. She kisses the baby on the head and walks over and hands him to Evan.

"Benny, hey buddy," Evan says as the baby reaches up to grab Evan's beard and squeals with happiness to see his dad. My heart expands in my chest when I think about how it must feel to have that. I want that. I get to have that.

"Hi," she says as she puts her arm around me.

"Want to have a picnic?" I tip my head down to hers and brush my lips across her cheek.

"Yes," she says as we make our way to an igloo and zip it behind us. "This is amazing. We get to stay in here tonight?"

"And we get to eat Sasha's food." I open the basket and pull out a thermos of soup and sandwiches wrapped in parchment paper.

"Say no more," she moans as she opens one of the sandwiches. "Homemade sourdough bread, thick-sliced turkey, Sasha's sandwich sauce, and soup? I'm in heaven."

"I thought it would be a fun date night," I admit.

"I agree. A good place for us to talk and spend time together," she says.

We sit in the chairs, and Holly props her feet up. We eat, chatting about the inn. "I had no idea it had been here for so long," I say.

"Yeah, Evan is the third-generation inn owner. They almost lost it last year. But Beth came and ended up helping Evan save it. They have a great story," she says as she looks out over the inn in the distance.

"You know the baby will be third-generation owner of Freedom Pie someday," I muse.

Her eyes grow misty. "I know. I think about that. We have a pretty great story, too. Don't we?"

"Our story's just beginning."

Beau

I come in through the back door of the restaurant, set down the groceries, and look around for Holly. I hear voices in the front of the restaurant and look out to see her chatting with Preston, her lawyer. It's our slow time, so the restaurant is deserted. I put the groceries away and can't help but overhear bits and pieces of their conversation. And parts of it make the hair rise on my arms.

"Signing over rights…"

"Protect your assets…"

"Relocating to Florida…"

I stand and take a deep breath, adjusting my ball cap, and grip the edge of the counter. What if she leaves?

I pour a glass of water and head out to the dining room. Preston and Holly pause and look up when I walk in. Not good.

"Everything okay?" I ask as I stand in the doorway.

"Yeah, almost done. Just working on some paperwork," Holly says as she grips a folder in her hands.

"How are you doing, Beau?" Preston asks.

"Great," I say quietly.

I know most of this isn't my business. Holly has been forthcoming on everything so far so now having secrets seems irrelevant. We've laid everything on the table up until now, or so I thought.

Preston looks at his watch. "I have to pick up Paige. We can finish this up another time. I'll see you later." Standing, he slides on his coat and waves.

"Thank you," Holly calls from the seat at the table as he heads out.

I look over at her. "You can't get up, can you?"

She shakes her head and laughs. "I'm stuck."

I reach an arm out and pull her gently from the booth, her belly close to the table. "What was Preston here for?"

"Just paperwork."

"Like for the surrogacy?" I ask.

"No, just in general." She shrugs as she stands and walks to the kitchen.

A bad feeling fills me when I think about Nadia and how

she screwed me over with everything. I don't think Holly would do that to me, but then I never thought Nadia would either. And this feels like something is going on here.

"Is there anything I need to know?" I ask as I put my hands on my hips and brace for whatever she might tell me. I can't shake this sense of doom, like something is off here. My chest feels tight, and my heart rate is erratic. I feel like at any point my world could come crashing down on me again, and this time, the stakes feel a lot higher. God, am I sabotaging myself? I suck in a deep breath and pull my hat off and nervously tuck it backward again.

"What do you mean?" she asks, turning to look at me.

"I mean, are you hiding anything from me? Is there something you're working on with Preston that I don't know about?" I question.

Her face freezes, and she looks at me with shock and surprise. "What are you talking about?"

"With Nadia..."

"Do I look like I'm Nadia? Beau, that's fucked up. I have been nothing but honest from the beginning with you."

"Really?" I challenge. "When I first moved here, did you or did you not plot to take the restaurant back from me?"

"I *offered* to buy the restaurant back from you," she says with disgust. "I never once tried to take something from you."

"How do I know you're not going to screw me over, too?" I

ask, but looking at her face, I know I've gone too far.

"You know, I think I'm going to get some fresh air," she says as she gathers her coat and purse, not looking at me. She looks crushed, and it absolutely guts me to see what I've done.

"Where are you going?" I ask, defeated.

"None of your fucking business, Beau," she snaps as she snatches open the door, heads out, and slams it behind her.

I throw my head back and sigh. I messed up. God, why do I always mess everything up? My shoulders sag in defeat. I have to fix this.

I flip the closed sign on the door and shut it between lunch and dinner. I need to take a walk. I need to figure out how to fix this.

I forgot my gloves and shove my hands down in my pockets and pull my hat lower. I kick a piece of snow, and it flies onto the street.

"What did that snowball do to you?" someone hollers. I look over and see SJ and Sam unloading tires from a semi-truck in front of Sam's Auto Body.

"Got in my way," I grumble.

SJ stands back and reaches into his back pocket and throws a pair of black work gloves at me. "Come work off your steam with me and Dad."

I catch the gloves and crack my neck. "Fine."

"What's got you mad?" Sam asks.

I shake my head. "I messed it up with Holly. Accused her of hiding stuff from me. I have a past with not trusting women and them using and screwing me over."

"Oof," SJ says, grimacing. "I've known Holly most of my life. And her family. She wouldn't do that."

"I don't know how I can fully trust anyone again," I say as I pick up a tire and load it inside the shop on the side of the wall. The smell of new tires permeates the air.

"Shit, we all have a past," Sam says. "Don't let your past get in the way of your future."

"Are you speaking from experience?" I huff as I pick up two more tires and stack them.

"Hell yeah. My ex fucked me over royally."

"What did she do?"

"Had an affair with another man, got pregnant with his baby, and tried to pass it off as mine. Then, when she couldn't fool me, she cut town, leaving SJ and me."

I pause and stare at him. "No shit. Seriously?"

He nods. "Yeah."

I look over at SJ, and he shrugs. "And the baby she had is my wife's half sister."

What in the Maury Povich?

"Okay, well, you guys win. That's some fucked-up shit," I

say with a shudder.

"We made it, and so will you," Sam says as he sets his pile of tires down.

SJ looks at me. "You can't let your past win. You want a future with Holly?"

"Yeah. I can't imagine not having her or the baby in my life now."

Sam nods. "If you didn't fight with her sometimes, it wouldn't be worth fighting for. And Holly is worth fighting for."

"How did you move on?" I ask Sam.

He shrugs. "Still working on that. Never met anyone I wanted to get serious with. So if you've found that with Holly, you better hang on to her."

Hang on to her. I can't imagine letting her go.

"Thanks for the talk," I say when all the tires are unloaded, and I hand SJ back his gloves. "Come by for a pie this weekend on me."

"I think we're supposed to be buying *you* dinner for helping." SJ laughs.

"Nah, I think I needed this more. Thanks," I wave as I head back to the restaurant. I needed this town. A place to call home and make a family.

My phone buzzes in my pocket, and it's Hank.

"What's up, Hank," I say, tired.

"You'd better get back here now," he says as I hear voices

raised in the background.

"What are you talking about?"

"Nadia is here."

Holly

Hank sits at the counter, sipping his drink. "All I'm saying is, he's been through some stuff."

"We all have, Hank. That's no excuse to be a dick to me when I did nothing wrong," I say as I pound the dough on the counter with my fist, angrily. When I went out for a drive, I ran into Hank, and he returned to Freedom Pie with me. He's been trying to talk me down from my fight with Beau. Luckily, Beau stepped out, so we've had the place to ourselves.

Hank says, "I know. Trust me, I'm the last person to make excuses for my sometimes-dumb brother."

"What am I supposed to do, Hank? He doesn't trust me."

"He does, he's just been screwed over. Give him a chance,

I'm begging you," he pleads.

Before I can answer, Charlie pops in from the dining room. "Hey, there's a lady here asking to see Beau. A Nadia?"

Hank's jaw drops, and his eyes narrow. Standing to his full six-foot-three height, he strolls to the dining room, and I grab a towel and follow him as quickly as I can. Which is more of a waddle.

I don't know Nadia, but I do know that she hurt the man I love, and his usually normal happy brother has basically come unglued, and I'm not having that. He would do anything for anyone he loves. Knowing she's here makes me feel like we have a rat in the restaurant, and it needs to be dealt with quickly. When I get to the dining room, I'm not sure what I expected, to be honest. But this woman is not it. She's surprisingly put together and cold.

A tall woman with bright red lipstick on stands in the front of the restaurant in an expensive-looking white coat, tall black boots, and perfectly curled, long dark hair. She's beautiful. I suck in a deep breath. So this is Nadia, Beau's ex.

She sneers at Hank, and her eyes narrow to slits. "What are you doing here?"

Okay. Now I really, really dislike this woman. I don't like the way she's looking and talking to Hank like that. I suddenly feel self-conscious next to her, but I can't shake the feeling of unease when I look at her. She may be a beautiful woman, but she's not a good person.

"What are you doing here, is the more pressing question, Nadia," Hank says as he squares up to her, hands on his hips.

I've never seen Hank angry like this, and I stand back and watch in fascination.

"Just go get Beau." She huffs.

"Just go get bent," Hank replies. He pulls out his phone and hits a few buttons, raising it to his cheek. He says something into the phone and disconnects, sliding it back into his pocket. He squares off and glares at Nadia.

My hand flies to my mouth, and I bark out a laugh, and her head snaps my way. "Who are you?"

I tilt my head with a smug smile. "Who are you?" I return.

"I'm Beau's wife," she says as she sucks in a breath and stands taller.

"The fuck you are. You are not his wife, and you need to run along," Hank says, walking to the door and motioning for her to leave.

"I'm not leaving until I see Beau."

I don't have the energy for this woman today. "Whatever you need to tell Beau, you can tell me, and I'll relay the message," I say firmly.

"And who are you?" she huffs. "Did you knock her up, Hank?"

Hank tilts his head and laughs. "No, she's Beau's."

Her eyes widen as she looks at my belly and at my face. "Not possible," she says with disgust. "He wouldn't downgrade like that."

Before I can get a word out, the door is open, and Nadia is out on the front walk, and Hank has the door locked behind her. He turns to me, his eyes bright and angry. "Now do you see what Beau had to live with? She does this. She screwed him over, and then the next guy she screwed over is probably gone, so she's back to screw with Beau again. He doesn't need that bullshit." He points his thumb at Nadia, who is trying to come back in the restaurant.

I nod, still shocked at Hank's maneuver. I look out, and she's on her phone. "I hope she's not calling the cops."

"I hope the fuck she is. I will get her for trespassing. I still legally own half this restaurant."

Still. What does that mean?

"Where the hell is she?" I swivel, and Beau stands in the doorway to the kitchen, looking just as angry as Hank. Jesus, what has this woman done to these brothers?

I look at the front of the restaurant where Nadia peers in the window and knocks, her phone still on her cheek, talking to someone.

Beau stares. "What the hell did she want?"

"She says she's your wife," I say as a feeling of heaviness comes over me just saying the words.

"She called Holly a downgrade," Hank offers in disgust.

"She needs to go. She is nothing to me, us, or this place." Beau looks at me and searches my eyes. "You are my *everything*, Holly."

Relief fills me that he's here and dealing with her.

Beau turns and walks to the door and calls through the glass, using his thumb to point. "Get gone."

"I just need to talk to you *alone*," she says as she glares at Hank and me.

"Not happening," Beau clips.

She takes a deep breath, and it's like she's fixing her invisible mask as she says, "I want a second chance."

Beau snorts. "Not a chance in hell. I have a great home and life here with my family. I'm truly happy, and I won't let you mess that up for us."

She looks at him like she's about to cry. "Beau, you don't mean that, honey. We share a past."

"We absolutely do have a past, and that's where you'll stay. I am not allowing you to shit on my future. Leave." Beau glares as he turns and stands next to me, pulling me into him.

She adjusts her purse strap and stares and then looks away, irritated that her plan didn't work.

"Leave while I'm feeling particularly nice about things, or I'll file a restraining order. Stay away from my family." Beau glares.

She looks riddled with anger and turns and walks away.

Good riddance.

Beau takes a deep breath and looks over at me. "You

okay?"

"I'm so sorry," I say.

"For what?" he asks, confused.

"That you had to live with that stale ham sandwich of a human being," I say, trying to make light of a stressful situation.

He shakes his head. "I'm sorry, Hol."

"I know," I murmur.

"I more than like you," he says as he wraps his hands around my belly and pulls me close, his mouth coming down to kiss my forehead.

"I more than like you back." I grin as I lean my forehead to his.

"There's nothing she could ever say to me," he says. "I had the wife, life, and restaurant. I did everything for Nadia. Apologized even when I shouldn't have and gave it my all. Even after all she did. So trust me when I say I gave up that seat for a reason. I do not care who sits after me. She and I have no business anymore."

I will always look at this man and wonder how any woman before me didn't see what I do. His unwavering loyalty to the people he loves or likes.

"Why do you smell like tires?" I ask, looking up at him, confused.

He smiles at me. "I was helping my new friends SJ and Sam."

Holly

Two missed calls are what I see when I finally get to my phone after a busy dinner rush that left me exhausted in a good way. The kind where your soul feels good, your cup feels full, and you just had a good day. For the most part. Something is missing with Beau. He's distant since we had our fight. He's been attentive as he always is, making sure that I eat, sit, and get off my feet and keeps my water bottle topped off.

But a strange distance is there between us. And I don't know how to fix it. Or if I can.

I flip through my notifications and see one missed FaceTime call and one missed call from my parents. Then a string of unread texts.

Mom: Just checking in, honey.

Mom: Let us know how you're doing. I heard you guys have had bad weather up there and just wanted to check in on you.

Dad: Let us know you're okay, love. We're just worried about you. Wish you would come down to visit.

Guilt pours through me and makes my veins run cold. How am I going to explain all this to them? I rub my temple and feel a tension headache coming on. I've put off telling them for so long that now I don't know how to fix the mess I've made with them. The distance between my parents and me is not something I'm familiar with. We've been close for my whole life, with the exception of travel and culinary school. Now that they're enjoying retirement down in sunny Florida, I feel estranged from them, and it makes me feel sad. I miss them. And things feel sad with Beau right now in some way. And this baby is coming, and I don't know how to get my life from feeling like it's veering off track at every moment. I feel like I'm just on this ride, and it's going where it wants to go. I have no control and no idea what's coming next.

I pick up the phone and call my mom and walk into the storage room and shut the door softly behind me. I sit on a big pallet of flour in the corner.

"Hi, honey," she answers cheerfully.

"Hi, Mom." I try to sound upbeat as well.

"Everything okay? We've been trying to get ahold of you." She sounds worried.

"Yeah, I'm fine. Just been busy with friends and work," I answer as I stifle a yawn.

"We worry about you. You're working so much. Still working all the jobs?"

"No, I cut back. I'm actually..." I clear my throat. "I'm actually working at Freedom Pie for the new owner."

You could have heard a pin drop on the line.

"You, what?" she asks, confused.

"I'm working as a co-chef at Freedom Pie," I admit quietly.

"Why?" she asks softly.

I can't help it, and heat pours to my eyes, and I start to choke up and cry. "Because I told you, Mom. I love this place, and I miss it. I was meant to be here, and this place feels like my home."

"Oh, honey," she says softly. "You have to move on. You can't stay trapped at the pizza place. You worked so hard there. Your dad and I don't want you to be tied to the restaurant life like we were. We want you to be happy. Go out and live your life."

"I am happy," I choke.

"Are you? You've been obsessed with the pizza place since you discovered we were selling it. You have talked nonstop about getting it back. This isn't healthy."

"That's not true, Mom." But is it? Is she right? I've poured my whole life in the past year into getting it back or starting over on my own. And I've even gone to lengths that are life-altering. What if I'm a bad person? What if Beau deserves better than a crazy person who just wants a pizza shop back? But I know that's not true because I've grown to love Beau and care so deeply about him. I want him more than I want the pizza place back. He's the unexpected in all of this. I fell in love with the person I couldn't have imagined falling in love with. I found my new friend Hank, who has become like a brother to me. They both mean so much to me.

"Your dad and I want to come up and check on you," she says, and I can feel her disappointment in her tone.

"No, Mom," I say quickly. "I'm fine, I told you. I...I gotta go. I'm fine, I promise. I'll call you in a few days." I can't tell her about the baby. There's no way that conversation will go well right now after just hearing I'm working here has sent her into a tailspin.

"We love you so much," she says with a small crack in her voice.

"I love you, too. I promise I'm good. I'm happy."

I straighten up and come out of the storage closet. Beau is carrying a tray of dishes and sets them in the sink. He sees my face, and his expression fills with worry. "What happened?"

I lean into his hug. "Just talked to my parents. They're worried about me and not happy I'm working here." A heaviness fills me, and I hate that my life has become one giant mess full of secrets.

"I think I'm going to drive out to the inn and see Sasha for a bit."

He looks at the clock and back at me. "It's late, let me drive you."

I shake my head. "The roads are clear, and I need the drive and just time to think."

He nods and crosses his arms. "Okay."

I can tell he's not happy, but he respects my space and hands me a water bottle as I head out.

I check on Stephen while my car warms. He's back in his little house above the porch and seems happy to be back outside now that the weather has cleared up. Beau scraped most of the snow off his roof, so he has room for his house. He curls into my arm and checks me over for food. "I'm sorry, Stephen. I don't have anything for you." He squeaks as he twitches his nose and crawls up my arm to perch on my shoulder. I move some of the snow by his house and pack it around so he'll stay warmer.

"Bye, buddy," I say softly as he trots into his house and curls up, his tail wrapping around his face as he drifts off to sleep again. "Sleepy squirrel," I murmur as I make my way to my now defrosted and warmed-up car.

I drive around town and admire the lights still strung up around the lampposts and the glimmer of the ice from the frozen lake in the middle of town. An ice-skating rink is set up under the pavilion, where we have a market in the summer. People are bundled up and having fun and smiling.

I pass through Main Street and take in all the decorated storefronts with the lights and signs bringing the street to life. Main Street has always been my favorite place in town. I pass Freedom Pie and wonder what Beau's doing. When I turn onto the road to the inn, peace fills me. The inn has always been the heart of Freedom Valley, and I always feel welcome here.

I open the front door, and immediately, the smell of food and the warmth from the fireplace and coffee hits me. I close my eyes in bliss. I shut the door, then peel off my gloves and stuff them in my pocket. My coat no longer zips, so I shrug it off, realizing I'm still in my chef coat and black pants.

Sasha comes down the hall, wiping her hands on a dishcloth, and sees me. "Holly, you're just in time for a slice of pie. Come on back," she calls.

I follow her and slide onto a stool at her counter. "Thanks, Sasha, it smells great in here."

"Did you eat? What brings you our way? This is a nice surprise."

"I just wanted to check in. I missed you guys."

"Things okay at Freedom Pie?" she asks curiously as she cuts two pieces of pie and slides a plate over to me.

"No, not really. Beau is great, but we just have some

distance right now. I don't know how to fix it. A lot is going on." I sniff.

She hands me a fork and slides onto the stool next to me. She says nothing, just sits and waits for me to continue.

"Sasha, I've made a mess of everything," I admit as I poke at my pie with my fork.

"What do you mean?"

"I told my mom that I was working at Freedom Pie, and she didn't like it. She doesn't want me to work there and doesn't understand that Freedom Pie is my passion. If she knew everything else, she'd think I'm nuts. I don't know how to come clean. I feel like if things are bad with my parents, I can't be happy with the baby and Beau and everything else. I feel lost." Tears stream down my face as I finally let everything out.

Sasha hands me a tissue and puts a hand on my back. "You've had a lot going on in a short time. A lot of life changes. Big ones. That's a lot to take in and digest."

"I know. I feel like I've had no time to really process how life will be now. What will life be like? How can I be a mom?"

Sasha smiles. "That I know you'll be great at, Holly. This baby is lucky to have you for a mom. It may not be how you thought things would go, but sometimes things work out and don't work out for a reason."

"What if Beau doesn't want me...us, and it becomes too much, and he leaves? Or I have to leave."

"I wouldn't worry about that. The way Beau looks at you is the way Pete looks at me, and that's a good man. And his brother Hank's just as lovely. If I had to add to my family, those guys would be at the top of the list. We all really like them around here."

I bite my lip. "What does Beau see in me? I have nothing to offer him. What if he thinks I'm with him just for Freedom Pie?"

Sasha laughs. "I had the same talk with Mellie when she met Ty. She was a single mom, too. And look at them. They're meant for each other. We all have that one person in the world meant for our souls. And when you meet them, you know. It doesn't matter if you've only known them for a minute, a week, or a year. The heart and soul know who its match is. Beau seems like he's your match."

Just thinking about Beau relaxes my body. I feel my phone buzz and pull it out of my pocket, and it's a text from him. I smile.

"That's him, isn't it?"

"Yeah. He wants to know if I'm doing okay." My fingers fly over my phone to text him back.

Me: Yes. Just having pie with Sasha.

Beau: Let me know if you want me to come get you. Have fun and be safe.

Sasha looks down at my phone and back at me. "That's what

love looks and feels like. Finding that person who just wants you to be safe and happy. You deserve someone like that, Holly."

"So does Beau," I murmur, thinking about how he's been screwed over and he just wants a family, not someone who schemed to buy back the restaurant to the point that I was willing to be a surrogate to get it back or build a competitive pizza business.

"Listen, you helped him with his restaurant when you didn't have to. You could have let him fail and probably lose it all. That's also what love feels like. It feels like helping others even when it doesn't exactly benefit you. You did what you did, and that means something."

"He would have figured it out."

"Maybe. But you have to admit, how cool is it that you made a miracle baby and met a man who is as passionate about Freedom Pie as you are?"

I chuckle. "Yeah, I guess."

"You get to raise your family at Freedom Pie and have a man who gets it and wants it just as bad as you do."

"You're right."

"It's snowing again. This winter has been insane. I've never seen New Hampshire get this much snow." She sighs as she looks out the window.

My phone buzzes.

Beau: Can I have pie, too? (Sad face)

Me: LOL Yes. Come to the inn. I miss you.

Beau: I'm already here. :)

I look over and see Beau's truck parked next to my car, the engine still running. "Beau wants pie."

Sasha looks at his truck and back at me. "Oh honey, it's not pie that man wants. It's you."

The back door opens softly, and Beau steps in, a black hat pulled over his head, bundled up, his soft green eyes on me, and then he turns. "Hi, Sasha."

"Come in. I heard you're after pie."

"Always after pie," he says as his eyes stare at me, and he looks relieved to see me.

I smile at him, and he comes over and wraps his big arms around me in a hug. He releases me and slides onto the stool next to me.

"You wanted Sasha's pie that bad?" I tease as I hold a forkful of pie, ready to bring it to my mouth when Beau swoops in. Gently taking my wrist in his big hand, he maneuvers the fork into his mouth. His eyes focus on mine as he wraps his lips around that bite of pie, savoring it, the tension palpable between us.

"That and I worried about you driving home in this," he says after he swallows my bite as Sasha slides a piece of pie across the table to him. He looks at it and says, "Apple is my favorite."

I pull my own plate closer and take a bite. This is it. Life with Beau and my friends. And pie. It may be a shit show, but this will do for now. It might just all work out. One bite of pie at a time.

CHAPTER 30

Holly

Beau has his arm around me as we head out to his truck. My car will never make it home in this weather, as I didn't plan for it to snow again, so we plan to come back for it. He has it all warmed up and helps me get in and buckled. He leans over and kisses me softly and then puts the truck in drive.

"We're going to need this four-wheel drive," he mutters as he pulls out.

"Are we good, Beau?" I ask him softly.

He looks over at me. "We're good. You have to understand that you're my world. That's my baby now. Ours."

I look at this man I probably don't deserve, but here he is. Mine. And I am overwhelmed and excited for the life we get to begin together here.

"I messed up when I tried to buy back Freedom Pie," I admit. "What happens if you get sick of me? Of us?"

"I will be here for you forever. I know you love Freedom Pie. I get it. I love it, too. We have the same dream, Holly. You don't want me? Tell me right now, and I'll leave you alone. But I think we want the same things. And I want it all with you, Holly."

I shake my head. "Don't leave."

"You're my family," he says as he leans over and kisses me. "You, me, this baby. Family. Oh, and my crazy brother. You've got him, too. We've got this."

"I more than like you so much," I say with a grin.

"I more than like *you* so much." He grins back.

I lay my head on his shoulder, my body relaxing.

"Don't ever doubt us. How we got here doesn't matter," he says softly.

"Do you think if I had never been pregnant, we still would have met?"

"It doesn't matter at this point. I'll love the baby as my own. I already do. And someday we'll add more to our family, and our family will be big, loud, and proud. That's what I can offer you, Holly. A loving family."

"I can't let you take on my crazy life. You raised Hank. What about your dreams? I want you to be happy."

"You are my dream," he says, his eyes staring into mine.

I'm finally starting to believe him. We're a family.

A few nights later, I wake up, and the moonlight pours in through the curtains. Beau breathes deeply next to me, fast asleep. Pain shoots through my core, and I sit up and hunch over the edge of the bed, gripping the mattress. Must be Braxton Hicks, I convince myself as I quietly head to the bathroom. Beau is asleep on his back, his face toward my side of the bed in the moonlight. Even sleeping, he's incredibly sexy. His face is relaxed, and his dark eyelashes fan his cheeks.

After I use the bathroom and wash my hands, I turn to head back to bed and feel a gush of warm fluid pour down my legs. I instinctively clench my legs and cry out in shock, hunching down.

I suck in a deep breath and look up to see the door yank open, and Beau frantically looks in. "Are you okay?"

"My water just broke. I'm having this baby tonight," I say with fear pulsing through me. I'm not ready. What if I can't do this? What if the pain is too much? I went through my entire pregnancy not really giving much thought to what happens when the baby actually comes, and all that fear and worry has sprouted out of nowhere when my water broke.

He nods. "Okay." He quickly reaches over and pulls a

hooded sweatshirt over his T-shirt. But the look on his face is far from okay. He looks about as terrified and excited as I feel right now. He pauses and looks at me. "Holly."

"What?" I ask, all my emotions swirling around and filling me with excitement, anticipation, and worry.

"We get to meet the baby!" he says, looking excited with a huge smile on his face.

Another contraction rages through my body, making me almost go to my knees.

Beau is on the move. He grabs the bag I packed last week just in case I went into labor, adding a few hygiene things from the bathroom, and brings them back in. My body tenses up with another contraction.

Beau waits, then helps me change. I want to be embarrassed, but I'm terrified, and I cling to him. "Beau, I want my mom. I need her."

He looks up at me. "I have it. Just breathe and focus on the baby. I won't leave you," he promises.

He's on the phone and looking out at the snow that has blanketed everything while we slept. The roads look snow-packed.

Another contraction rolls through me, and Beau looks at his watch and back at me. Worry fills his eyes.

"What?" I ask, starting to panic.

"We're snowed in," he says, his ear still to the phone.

Beau

"This storm was worse than the last. Plows are even struggling, can't keep up," Hank says on speakerphone.

"How is that even freaking possible? They said nothing about this!" I say as I pace nervously.

"How far apart are her contractions?" Hank asks.

I look over as another one takes over Holly's body. She tightens up and looks at me, her face twisted in pain.

"Close."

"Shit," Hank mutters. "Hold on." He covers the phone and talks to someone in the background.

I reach for Holly's hand, and she squeezes it, nodding through the contraction while looking at me in fear.

"Okay, we're coming in the big rig fire truck. It has snow tires. All the ambulances are out on runs. Get ready. We'll get her to the hospital. It's the best we can do," he says.

"Thanks," I disconnect and carry her down the stairs.

"I'm a horrible daughter," she cries. "I should have told my parents. I want my mom."

"No, you're not. It'll be okay. Just breathe and focus on the baby. I'll call your mom and dad."

But I'd be lying if I didn't admit that I'm scared shitless. She's having a baby, and I'm so worried. I want her mom to come. Hell, I really wish my mom was here.

She breathes through a few contractions, and I time these, and they're happening quick. Her eyes are full of fear as they dart to mine, and I can tell she's probably thinking the same thing.

"I'm here. I've got you." I kiss her head and hold her through it. She grips my hand and holds it as we hear sirens approaching on Main Street. Hank and a bunch of firefighters come in and set down a gurney and evaluate her. One of the firefighters looks up and says the contractions are very close, you might want to check her. Hank goes around, and Beau grabs him. "Absolutely not."

He rolls his eyes. "It's my job, Beau," he reminds me.

Lola waves them off and checks Holly. "I can see the head."

Oh my God.

"NO! Please! I can't have my baby here. I need a hospital,"

she pleads.

"Let's get her going," Hank says as he picks Holly up and hands her to another firefighter who makes a seat in the truck as comfortable as they can for Holly.

"It's okay," I reassure her as I follow them and jump in the truck, helping her lay across the seats, tucking her into me.

"I didn't know your fire truck doubled as an ambulance," I joke. I'm trying to play it cool for Holly, but I'm feeling nervous.

"It absolutely does not, but for my brother, it does," Hank says as he slides in. The sirens start, and we trudge along to the hospital. If the fire truck can barely make it, my truck wouldn't have made it, let alone Holly's car.

I look over at my brother and give him a small smile.

He nudges me with his shoulder. "Let's go make you a dad."

A dad.

I've wanted to become a dad more than anything in the world. I want to have a little kid to take to the movies. Backyard birthday parties. Family vacations. A vision of driving my truck and hearing a little voice chattering to me from the back seat. I want to spend Christmas Day assembling toys and having big family dinners that end with too much food and so many laughs. I want it all with Holly. *I get to have this*, I think to myself, feeling like the luckiest guy in the world.

I can't even tell you how I got here, but I know that this is where I'm meant to be. We're not a typical family, but nothing in my life has been typical. I've spent most of my life waiting for the other shoe to drop. I'm not doing that anymore. I've been given a new shot with Holly, and I'm taking it.

I went through my business paperwork and saved Holly's parents' information in my phone in case of an emergency. The first chance I get, I'll be calling her parents. They need to be here. We have a lot of explaining to do, but if Holly wants them here, she gets them here.

When the fire truck pulls up to the hospital, a team is waiting for us. Holly is pulled out and placed on a stretcher and moved quickly inside, Hank and I following close. I'm relieved that we're here, and she didn't end up delivering in the fire truck or the apartment.

"Beau," she calls nervously.

"I'm here!" I call as I jog behind to keep up.

"Don't leave me," she begs.

"Not a chance I'd leave you," I say as a moan and small scream come from Holly.

Holly is moved to a hospital bed, and it's set up quickly as a doctor wearing a mask pulls on gloves and a gown.

"You got here just in time, Holly," he says as he checks her. "It's a great day to have a baby."

"It's a snowstorm out there," she breathes, and her face

twists in pain. "What's so great about it?"

"Babies don't wait for snowstorms," he says as he prepares for the birth.

Hank and I are up by Holly's head, and we each hold one of her hands. I stroke her hair, and her flushed cheeks are bright red as her eyes search for mine. She stares at me and nods, almost like she's trying to convince herself she can do this.

I nod back to her, trying to reassure her.

"Alright, which one of you is the dad?" the doctor asks, looking back and forth between Hank and me.

"I am," I say confidently as I look at Holly, and she gives me a small smile and pants.

"Do you want to cut the cord?" he asks.

"Right now?" I ask nervously.

"It'll be soon." He chuckles.

"Yes," I say as I look at Holly, her eyes not leaving mine as she focuses.

"You've got this, Holly," Hank encourages, patting her arm.

"Don't look at anything, Hank," she pants.

Hank shakes his head and laughs. "Not a chance in hell I'm looking down there. I'm staying right up here."

A nurse steps in and begins to prepare a baby bed and set up supplies. This feels *very* real all of a sudden.

"Alright, Holly, are you ready? I think we're close," the

doctor says behind his mask as he turns and says something to the nurses.

Holly's eyes meet mine, desperately searching for something, and when I give her a reassuring smile, she seems to relax.

"It's okay. You can do this," I murmur.

"Okay, give me one big push, Holly," the doctor says as I hold Holly's hand and Hank holds her other hand.

Holly closes her eyes, and her chin goes to her chest. A few tears slide out from the corners of her eyes, and she squeezes my hand tightly.

The room is quiet for a minute, and a tiny sound that almost sounds like a baby kitten fills the room, a baby cry. The doctor places the baby on Holly, and we all look down, tears streaming down Holly's face. "Ohhhhh," she says softly.

"It's a girl," I whisper as we stare at her squished-up, howling pink face.

"She already cries like you," Hank says as he looks at the baby, and I can tell he's emotional as well.

I look at him and squint my eyes. "She's perfect."

"Yeah, she is," he says softly as he gazes at the baby.

I kiss Holly's forehead as she looks at me like she's going to melt with emotions. "You did great, Momma. She's perfect." She's exhausted, but her eyes are lit up as she takes in and examines the baby as I witness her eyes falling in love with her. Holly is the most beautiful woman I've ever seen, and

I'm so grateful she let me be with her for our baby's birth. I choke back emotion as I look at Hank, and he says, "Hell yeah, Brother. Hell yeah." He claps me on the back. Both of us are emotional, blinking back tears.

"Look at her, Beau," she says softly as she holds the blanket back.

"I see her. She's so beautiful, just like her momma." I lean down and gaze at both of my girls.

My family.

Holly's sleeping, and the baby is curled up on my chest, covered in blankets as I make a very important phone call.

"Hello," Maris answers.

I clear my throat. "Hi, Maris, this is Beau Sutton. I bought Freedom Pie from you."

"Yes," she says hesitantly. "Is everything okay?"

"Everything is okay," I reassure her. "but I need you and Frank to return to Freedom Valley as soon as possible."

The baby stirs on my chest and makes a little noise.

"Why?" she asks, alarmed.

"Because I need you to meet your granddaughter."

The line was quiet for a few beats, and then she says, "I'm sorry?"

"Holly wanted me to call you. It's a long story, but she's

asked me to fill you in so you have a little time to process before you get here." I tell Holly's mother everything that has happened with the surrogacy, right through Holly and I being together. "She was so brave going through labor. You would have been so proud of her. But she was emotional and asked for her mom. She needs you."

"Oh my God. Frank!" she yells.

I smooth my hand down the baby's back and cup her tiny head.

"Where is she?"

"Freedom Valley Memorial. She's sleeping right now, but I know she wants you here and regrets not telling you sooner."

"We're coming."

Holly

I didn't miss the tears in Beau's eyes when he was handed our baby when they wheeled me back to my room from labor and delivery. He followed, carrying our baby swaddled in a pink blanket in his arms. A baby girl.

Even Hank didn't leave and sat in his uniform in the corner with Beau, who looked deliriously tired but happy. He hasn't left our side and has been bringing us snacks, food, and checking in with the nurses.

I felt cold and tired, and Beau gave the baby to Hank to hold for a minute and climbed in beside me in my hospital bed and wrapped his arms around me, holding me. The only thing that could make this better is to have my mom here, but I messed up by not telling them. A tear falls on my cheek as I think about them.

The following day, I wake up from a nap and look over to find Beau and Hank fighting over who's going to hold her. Beau says, "She's mine, give her to me."

Hank frowns at him. "She's all of ours, dummy. I'm her uncle Hanky."

"*Never* ever call yourself that again," Beau grumps.

"Ew, what's that smell?" Hank says as he pretends to throw up.

Beau smiles smugly. "Why don't you check her diaper and find out."

I look over and see them staring at her with a mixture of disgust and awe. I hold back a laugh, watching them. These two pizza brothers came in and turned my world upside down. And now they're my family. My found family. And I couldn't imagine not having them both in my life. Our life now.

A knock on the door and then it opens, and my parents come pouring in, looking around with balloons and flowers in their arms.

"Mom," I start to cry, scared of what she's going to say. My dad comes around and puts his arm around me.

"I see you've been busy, honey," she says with an emotional smile. But I can tell she's not mad. She's happy to see me.

"I'm so sorry, Mom. I made some mistakes," I whisper.

"Shhh. We're here now, and we'll help you with anything you need. Look at your baby," she whispers proudly as Beau comes over and gently places her in my mom's arms now with a fresh diaper.

Hank comes over and shakes my dad's hand. "Congratulations, Grandpa. I'm Hank. Beau's brother." My dad looks happy to meet him and pulls him in for a hug, clapping him on the back.

I look over as my dad wipes his eyes, looking down at my mom and daughter.

"I'm a grandma," she says in awe, looking at him and back at me. My mom glows with a Florida tan and a mile-wide smile, and she looks so happy. I'm so glad they're here. I look over at Beau and mouth, "Thank you."

"I wanted to tell you," I start.

My dad holds up his hand. "Beau filled us in. Quite the young man you have there," he says proudly, reaching out to shake Beau's hand. Then Dad pulls him into a hug, patting him on the back. Beau looks proud, relieved, and happy to have them here all at the same time. My chest warms with how amazing Beau is. I don't deserve him, but here he is.

Beau comes around and puts his arm around me as my

parents look at our baby.

"What's her name?" my mom asks, looking up.

I look at Beau and swallow. "Claire."

Beau sucks in a deep breath, and his hand clenches over mine. His mother's name. Hank comes over and gives me a hug. "I love it," he whispers.

Another knock appears and our social worker Betty Cranmore comes in with her purse over her shoulder, carrying her clipboard. "How's Momma and baby?" she asks with a wide smile.

She comes in and takes in our family, nodding and smiling. "A happy family," she decrees, pulling out her notebook.

"I have a form here you can sign. I've seen everything I need to see here, and this is a beautiful family. This baby is lucky to have you all."

I hurry to scribble my signature and hand it back to her. "I'm proud of you, honey. Take care, and I'll see you Friday at Freedom Pie." She winks as she heads out and shuts the door softly.

I look at Beau, and his forehead dips to mine.

CHAPTER 33

Beau

We've been home a week now. I told Holly she could have the restaurant as long as I get her and Claire. She told me that's not necessary and that it's all of ours. I'd give Holly anything she wants. She wants the moon and stars? I'll build a fucking ladder and go get them for her.

Maris and Frank have been busy helping out wherever they can with the restaurant. They bought out Hank's part of the restaurant and gave it to Holly. Preston handled everything. It's officially ours. Our family's new legacy. Claire's future if she wants it. I think they felt bad about how they sold it and wanted to make it right after talking to Hank, Holly, and me. They didn't have to do that, but I think it made Holly feel like they believe in her now and her dreams with the restaurant, and I want that for her. She seems so happy now, like all is right with her world, and she deserves that. I want everything for her. Family means everything to me, and I want her family around. I'd give anything to have my own family around. I may not have my parents, but I'm making the family I dreamed of and missed.

I've fallen head over heels in love with not only Holly but also baby Claire. They are now marked on my soul forever. And I really like Maris and Frank. They were excited to be back at Freedom Pie and have been a huge help.

Claire stirs as she sleeps on my chest, and I rub her back. She's in her baby carrier, and I insist on wearing her, always keeping her close to me when she's not with Holly. I never knew I could have such a deep love for another human being. I love this baby and Holly with all my soul. She may not be biologically mine, but she's *mine*.

Maris and Frank stayed and ran the restaurant while we settled in with Claire. I try to go downstairs and help, but they always shoo me off to rest with Holly, taking the baby so we can eat, sleep, and Holly can recover. She's been trying to figure out how to breastfeed with Beth helping her.

This town has stepped up even more for Holly and me. A meal train or whatever it's called has been set up, and food just magically appears every day at our apartment. I think everyone forgets we have a restaurant, but it's been nice to be able to feed visitors quick and easy meals. Since the storm has passed and people are able to get out and around again, they are all putting in pizza orders and are excited to stop by and catch up with Holly's parents. They're staying at the inn, so they've been able to catch up with the Harpers, too. They show up every morning and work until close. I've loved getting to know them.

I can tell Holly is happy her parents are here. I take Claire up to Holly so she can feed her, and as I tiptoe into the dark bedroom, Claire whimpers, and Holly stirs from her nap. "She's hungry, Hol."

"I'll take her." She reaches for her. "How are things downstairs?"

"Well"—I run a hand over my face—"your dad rearranged all our spices, so that will probably take a while to figure out. Oh, and guess what?" I exclaim proudly.

"What?" she says as she stares over at me.

"Your dad taught me the secret family sauce recipe. He says I'm in the family now, so I get to know it." I do a fist pump. I'll admit, him teaching me that recipe was the highlight of my day, to feel included like that.

"Are you serious?" she says. "Things must be going really well, then. Now you can make all of the sauce batches," she teases.

"Your mom has been cooking up a storm and freezing extra meals. I don't think she realizes we run a restaurant and will never go hungry, along with the other meals that have been dropped off. She claims she's waited twenty-seven years to become a grandma, and she's not missing anything. Honestly, it's been nice. And your parents have this place down. I miss having parents," I admit.

"You have parents now," she says softly, her hand reaching to cup my face.

"My parents would have loved you both," I admit as I stare at her and Claire. "And my mom would be so happy to have a baby named after her."

"I still feel guilty for not telling them everything sooner," she says.

"It's okay. It all worked out. They're doing good with it all."

"Yeah. Beau?"

"Yeah?"

"I love you," she says in the dark.

"I love you both more."

"Impossible," she murmurs.

I lie beside them and hold my family.

CHAPTER 34

Holly

Seven weeks later...

The sun streams in, and it's Monday, our lazy day as a family when the restaurant is closed. Beau and I bask in the sunlight that streams in, covering our naked bodies in light. Beau kisses me down my collarbone and up my neck.

"I love you," he whispers so as not to wake a sleeping Claire in the next room. The monitor is still quiet, thankfully.

"I love you more," I say back as he pulls me to him, kissing him deeply. My Beau, my love. The man who makes me feel like we can take on anything together.

I snuggle into him, and he pulls me closer, the feeling of spring already in the air. Not quite ready to open the windows and let the fresh air in, but close.

"What are our plans for the day?" Beau asks as he twines our fingers together and kisses the back of my hand.

"Hank's coming over for brunch, and we're going to the inn later. Mellie has been working on her greenhouse, and I want to help her," I say, closing my eyes, deep in bliss lying here snuggling with Beau.

"We still have time…" Beau murmurs as he nuzzles my neck, and I wrap my arms around his neck.

Being with Beau has been everything and more than I ever could have imagined. Life is busy, full, and fun. I love every moment that we have. We've built a life that I love and look forward to every day.

My parents returned to Florida a few weeks after Claire was born, claiming they needed to give us space in our new life. They seemed sad to go but said they'll be back when we're ready for them again. We've already made plans to go to Florida when Claire's a little older. My parents can't wait to show Claire off to all their new friends. We're already planning a trip and excited to see them again.

I'm so thankful we were able to spend the time we had together. And my parents not only gained a granddaughter but Hank and Beau as well. They absolutely loved Hank and

Beau. My mom agreed with me that it's funny how fate has brought us together.

Hank sits at the kitchen table and plays on his phone while drinking his coffee. I go to the fridge to find the Mason jar I've been pumping breast milk into and turn to find it on the table next to Hank's mug.

"Hank, that's breast milk," I say quickly as he's taking a sip, and he sprays coffee everywhere.

"Gross," he says, wiping his tongue with his napkin. "Why didn't you tell me?"

Beau doubles over in the doorway, laughing. "How's your coffee, Hank?"

"Shut up, Beau." Hank side-eyes him, a grossed-out look still on his face.

"Did you hear that the surrogacy agency shut down?" Beau asks me.

"I saw they emailed," I say with relief. "I think it was a final email letting us know that we're done. J27 gave us the best gift ever. We are free from all of that now, according to Preston."

"What did you just say?" Hank asks in a tone that makes Beau and I turn and look at him.

"I was saying that everything is done with the surrogacy agency. And it shut down."

"No, what did you say about J27?" Hank says, eyes wide.

Beau's eyes shoot at him. "You did not."

Hank nods.

"You donated your sperm?" Beau shouts, his eyes wide in horror. "You're fucking with us right now."

"J27 was my donor. Are you sure that's you," I say, still waiting for Hank to confirm that he's messing with us.

Hank stares at us.

"I'm going to kill you," Beau says.

But when I look at Hank, I finally see that he's joking and unable to hold it back.

Beau looks like he's ready to freak out, and when he sees Hank's face, he rolls his eyes. "Dickhead."

"Gotcha," Hanks says.

"You're on shitty diaper duty," Beau demands.

Hank backs away, holding up his hands. "I was just joking! I'm still not changing poopy diapers," Hank says as he walks over to stare down at Claire.

He and Beau look at each other and clap each other on the back in a hug.

"What's happening?" I look between them, making sure they're not going to punch each other while holding Claire.

"Poopy diapers," Beau says with disdain. "You're getting all of them."

Holly

"I can't believe they get along," Paige says as she takes a sip of her sangria at my baby shower at the bookstore.

"Me, neither," I say as I sit in an easy chair at the bookstore, watching Stephen and Pancake wrestle in the corner.

"Do you think it's weird that we have wild animals for pets?" Paige muses.

"Yes," Beth and Allie say at the same time. "But at this point, if it wasn't weird, it wouldn't be our lives."

"Are they really wild, though? Maybe Stephen is, but Pancake is practically a dog at this point." I grin.

"What do you think the guys are doing?" Mellie asks as

she pours everyone more sangria.

"Preston has been smoking brisket and ribs all day for their get-together," Paige says.

"That sounds really good, actually," Mellie says with a deep sigh. "I miss Ty."

"We could crash their party and steal all their food." Allie shrugs. "They're just at the barn."

"I like our food," I admit as I look at the table filled with slider sandwiches, sangria, and various side salads. "Thank you for throwing me a baby shower."

"Of course, Claire needs to be celebrated," Beth says as she sets her plate down.

"If you could go back a year ago and see where you are today, would you believe it?" I ask all of them, thinking about the past year for all of us.

Beth laughs. "It wasn't that long ago that I broke down outside of town, and Evan found me and brought me back to the inn."

Mellie looks thoughtful. "It wasn't long ago that Evan brought Kase and I back to the inn, too. Didn't he used to call us his strays he collected?"

Allie laughs. "Whatever it was, I'm glad you're all here. I can't imagine not having you all in our lives."

Paige raises her eyebrows. "Life rarely turns out the way we plan. Coming back and opening the bookstore and finding Preston has been the best thing that could have happened to me."

The front door to the bookstore bursts open, and Evan, Logan, Ty, Preston, SJ, Hank, and Beau come pouring in carrying foil-covered containers and chattering.

"We're crashing this party!" Hank exclaims as he kisses Ophelia on the cheek, who is sitting beside me.

"Oh good, you brought the meat," Beth says, excited.

Allie and Mellie cover their mouths in giggles.

"Dirty birds," I tease.

"We did," Preston says as he sets the containers on the table, sliding down a few side dishes. He then leans down and kisses Paige.

"Hi," I say to Beau, who leans down to look at Claire in my arms and kisses me on the cheek.

"We missed you guys. We also got bored and thought we would combine the parties," Evan says as he sits beside Beth and steals a slider sandwich off her plate.

Beau glances over at the corner and back to me. "What is Stephen doing here?"

"He's having a playdate with Pancake." I shrug.

Beau looks at the ceiling and takes a deep breath. "This is a strange life we live."

"That's what I said," Beth agrees.

Hank's in the other room with Ty, plugging in a slow cooker of food, and I look at Ophelia and say, "So when are you two going to make it official?"

"Well, he's been trying to make it official," Ophelia admits.

"What's holding you back? He's not like Nial, you know."

Evan's eyes narrow. "Fuckin' Nial. I wish we knew where that asshat was."

"Axel told me the club handled him. I'm not worried about Nial anymore," Opi says as she sighs with relief.

"If the club took care of Nial, maybe we *should* be worried about Nial." Ty laughs.

"Opi is too nice. I'd love five minutes alone in a room with Nial and a hammer."

"Being nice is overrated. Just have a good lawyer and choose violence." Allie shrugs.

Preston looks over and shakes his head. "No violence."

"Why? We'll have you as our lawyer," Ty says.

Preston takes a sip of sangria. "Don't make more work for me."

Ophelia is now standing with Hank, playfully arguing. Hank looks at her and says with a teasing grin, "Shut your mouth."

Ophelia looks up at him and says defiantly. "Make me."

"Make you what, a mom?" he says in a flirting voice as he leans in and kisses her neck.

I love seeing my friend happy with Hank. I couldn't have picked a better man for her if I had tried. They're perfect for each other.

Beau leans in and takes Claire from me, curling her into

his arms. "How's our little lady?" He looks at Claire so lovingly it practically makes me melt.

"Who is next to have a baby or get married?" SJ asks as he looks around.

"Not me." Callie shakes her head.

"All set here," Allie claims.

"When are you going to marry me?" Hank says to Ophelia in a teasing way.

Ophelia shrugs, but her mouth is inches from him, whispering something that makes him blush.

"Oh yeah?" he mutters.

"You can't change me, Hank. I am who I am," she teases.

"I've learned with you, Ophelia, is that I would never want to change anything about you. Except your last name. Your attitude and smart mouth aren't going anywhere."

She playfully swats him, but he leans down and kisses her softly.

I look at Beau, and he puts his arm around me. "I love that for him," he murmurs to me.

"Yeah," I say.

Logan looks at Allie. "When are you going to tell them?"

Allie and Logan whisper something quietly, and the room waits for them to say something.

Evan tilts his head in question. "What's up?"

Allie says, "I was waiting to make it official, but now I can. Last year, I applied to a baking reality TV show and got chosen. They're going to film a small TV series here at Baked Inn Love and have a bake-off competition. We start filming this spring."

"Whoa! That is amazing, Allie, I'm so excited for you," Mellie says as she gives Allie a hug.

"Wow, my sister is famous," Evan says with a high five for his sister.

"Thanks, I'm pretty excited. It's kind of a hush-hush type of thing. Logan and I signed a contract, and I can't say too much about it yet. So don't tell anyone yet," Allie says as she leans into Logan. He places an arm around her, pulling her close.

Ty and Mellie are seated together, and I notice she's drinking ice water and not sangria like everyone else. "Hey, Mellie," I say, nodding to her water and grinning at her. "You okay?"

She grins and looks at Ty. "Anything to share with the class?" I whisper.

She nods and looks at me and the group. My eyes widen, and I suck in my breath through my teeth. "Really?"

"Ty and I have a little announcement," Mellie says as she looks at Ty, and the only way I can describe her face is the heart-eyed emoji.

"This summer, we're going to have a new addition," Ty says proudly.

"I'm so happy for you guys," Paige says. "We get to plan

another baby shower."

"Just do a joint one, this time. You know we'll just join you anyway," Logan says.

"We can do a spring barbecue at the inn," Evan offers.

"Yes," Mellie says. "I'd love that."

"Congratulations, guys!" I say with a smile.

A new generation of Freedom Valley is happening, and I'm so thankful for these people I get to call my family.

The End.

ALSO BY ERIN BRANSCOM

FREEDOM VALLEY SERIES

Falling Inn Love

Baked Inn Love

All Inn Thyme

All Inn Books

Forever Inn Love

Snowed Inn

NON-FICTION

Writers Inspiring Writers with Jennifer Probst

ABOUT THE AUTHOR

Erin Branscom has read everything she can get her hands on for as long as she can remember. To this day, her favorite place is still the library. In 2021, after a decade of writing novels just for fun, she finally decided to finish a book series and has found writing novels to be her greatest escape. Erin is a passionate author's advocate and loves sharing books on all her platforms. She lives in Oklahoma and loves gardening, traveling, and spending time with her husband, four kids, and best friend Molly, a Boston Terrier mix and her new edition, Love, an ornery blue heeler.

Website: Erinbranscom.com

Mailing list: bit.ly/3Z0QbV2

TikTok: @mylevel10life

Bookbub: @erinbranscom

Goodreads: www.goodreads.com/mylevel10life

Facebook: @erinbranscomauthor

Facebook Reader Group: Erin's Reading Nook

Instagram: @mylevel10life

Email: erin.branscom@gmail.com

ACKNOWLEDGEMENTS

Dusty, Kameron, Ethan, Audrey, and Charlotte, thank you for being the best family I could ever ask for. Thank you for always supporting me on my crazy adventures. I love you all so much!

Avi, you're a great kid and I'm so glad we get to have you in our lives.

Mom, thanks for reading my books and encouraging me. You're the best mom.

Dad and Michael in heaven, I miss you both so much. Every day. It's not fair. I wish you were here. I hope I've made you proud.

Julie and Elizabeth, thanks for being great sisters. We've been through so much in the past few years. Our family is still standing strong.

Auntie Susan and Auntie Paula, you are the best aunts anyone could ever ask for. I love you both so much.

Molly, you are my best friend in the entire world. Thanks for listening to me talk about all this book stuff and for always keeping me warm in my chair. You deserve all the bones and snuggles. I'm so sorry I keep bringing home more dogs. You know you're always my #1.

Brianna, I couldn't do it all without you! Thank you so much!

Erica, you're my favorite human. Period.

Kristi, your taco dates, and brainstorming sessions mean the world to me. I'm so thankful for you and your friendship. Also, your success is so inspiring. You work harder than anyone I know!

Nicole and Jenny, thank you for making this book the best that it could be!

Enni (Yummy Book Covers), thank you for bringing Freedom Valley to life. I love all these covers so much! Thank you for all that you do!

Laura, thank you for being the best alpha reader and giving me real feedback that challenges me to always do better.

To everyone reading this... Thank you for taking a chance on me and my Freedom Valley world.